Nyifie Brothers Publishing

FUTURE PROOF

A Stand-Alone Novel in the World of The Beam

JOHNNY B. TRUANT

SEAN PLATT

FUTURE PROOF

Chapter One

GIGO

IN TWENTY-FOUR HOURS, all but one of them would be dead. Maybe it was because of the box, maybe because of what the box turned out to be, or maybe because the mission itself was flawed even before Ryu believed he'd planned it. Only in retrospect were flaws in the system obvious. At the start there were eleven of them, and their aggregate goal was simple — noble, even. As individuals, they were more complex. All were codeboxes in human form, each with their own ones, their own zeroes, their own 512-bit encryption keys. That was the thing some of them missed and those who should have known better forgot: with enough intel you could control the game, but chaos was baked into the players. Biology began with amino acids in a sequence, transcribed from RNA in a sequence. They should have seen it coming. They'd accounted for everything, but forgot that life itself was a cypher.

Chapter Two

SAVAGE

Buzzed haircut, five-four in boots, arms like a climber and mouth like the floor of a tavern, Savage would probably have run the operation if it wasn't Ryu who'd brought the group an offer none of them could refuse. She wasn't angry to be another of the guns, but Twilight, the only other woman, was mad on her behalf.

In Twilight's view, Ryu only held the reins because he had a dick. Savage was more practical. She thought Ryu was in charge because the man kept his ear to the ground and his nose to the wind. He knew all the others, or at least their reputations. He was the one who'd discovered the changeover, or at least that's what they all believed at the time.

Savage had killed her share of men. She didn't kill Ryu because he mattered apart from his man parts. Besides. If dicks were so important, anyone could get one installed. Or two. Replace all ten fingers and it wouldn't raise your status a knot. God knew the gutterpunks in Little Harajuku had done stranger things, and nobody was handing them any promotions.

Equality this far from the turn of the millennium was, in Savage's mind, about other things: merit maybe one-fifth of the equation, social hierarchy the remaining four. The arrangement might have been okay if the nation knew the hierarchy existed, but that right there was the problem.

That's what they'd come to fix, and Savage for one planned to do her part to make it happen.

A share of the haul was just icing on the cake, and that investment kept growing without attention or effort. Her share had bumped twenty percent in the last fifteen minutes … and although she didn't know it yet, that take was about to jump another twenty-five.

That was another problem with the plan: the incentives were all wrong. Keeping your teammates alive meant splitting the pot into more pieces. Death, on the other hand, was the best way to boost your bottom line — assuming that bitter end belonged to someone else.

Tenor was covered in blood. Not his own, but in retrospect it should have been a sign. Savage was furious at him for it. Noah Fucking West … couldn't Tenor do anything right?

"You ass," she said. "Get your clothes off. And drop them in the incinerator."

Tenor tried to roll his eyes, so Savage shoved him hard. Twilight wasn't entirely wrong; testosterone made these XYs more confident than they should be, whereas women had to summon actual reasons for things. Savage had to hit people more often than most to keep her respect when adrenaline ran high.

At least she enjoyed it.

"I told you not to touch him. I fucking *told* you, Tenor."

"He was bleeding out."

"Yeah. *Out.* You bleed *out* when you're dying, not when it's worth risking everyone's life for some goddamn warm fuzzies. What are you, a priest? You should have kept your fucking hands to yourself. Now look."

She pointed. Tenor looked, dripped blood, and laughed. Of course he couldn't see the trail. Locus's specs would've caught it, and Savage saw it because she'd installed the eyes Ryu had sold her.

But to Tenor, the path he'd crossed from the door would look exactly like the floor of a standard scatter pod. To him it was proof that Savage was paranoid. That she was behaving irrationally. He was the kind of guy who believed that those things he couldn't see would never be able to hurt him.

"Your stupid micro-detritus is going to lead them right to us," Savage said, ignoring his mockery. "What if they have swarms?"

Ryu shook his head. "They don't have swarms. This is DZPD we're talking about, not a bunch of NPS agents."

"Just do it," Savage told him, jabbing Tenor toward the incinerator. "Burn your shit or someone'll sniff it out eventually."

"Yeah. *Eventually*."

"Clothes off or we've got a problem." She looked to Daemon and Twilight for support, but only Twilight managed to give it. Daemon was wrist-deep in mission electronics, doing his magic when it was no longer precisely needed. When Savage stared pointedly in his direction, his facial expression said, *Who, me?*

Tenor shrugged. "Look, Savage — if you wanna fuck me, just say so."

When she didn't bite, he scoffed and started to strip off his blood-soaked clothes, standing nowhere near the incinerator's catch pad. Jesus. They'd have to hire a crew of underground scourers to get the DNA out of this place, and all because some assholes couldn't follow directions.

The door banged. Savage drew her weapon and spun to aim it, but anyone unauthorized would enter using a ram or piston. A Ryu lock couldn't be opened by force unless there was a metric ton of it.

The newcomers were Ryu and Locus, upright, holding an injured Asp between them. Shot in the leg by what looked like a conventional round, judging by the size of his wound. A slamgun would have knocked his foot off like a bowling ball hitting pins, and nobody back there was using slumbers.

The fact that security was using lead-slug ammunition was a bit of panic that Savage hadn't allowed herself to think too much about yet. DZPD, who they'd anticipated, would have used slams or slumbers. Same for registered, legal security. The only real reason to use bullets was shooting at will without anyone metering the shots. Energy weapons could be muted from a distance. But not so when it was all primer and gunpowder. That little difference would, when time allowed, make Savage wonder who exactly was handling security at Xenia Labs if not official guards.

But right now she had no time to ponder.

Tenor laughed again, then buttoned himself back up. He didn't understand that bleeding your own blood was different from trailing someone else's, especially when nano swarms were involved. She'd need to do something about Tenor. Knock him out, maybe, assuming Ryu agreed.

Chase was behind them, carrying Asp's gear for him.

He dropped it and said, "Time to fly." He had a Wild East accent. Savage supposed it was sexy.

"Five minutes," said Ryu.

"In five minutes they'll be all over us. Time to fly."

Ryu didn't answer this time. He and Locus dragged

Asp to where Savage and the others were standing, then lowered him into a chair.

"What happened," Savage asked. It was more a statement than a question, delivered in military fashion.

Locus looked up. With those black specs permanently on his eyes, he looked like an insect. A very cool, very muscular bug.

"Same guy that got Smoke. I guess he wasn't dead."

"Smoke's dead?" It was Twilight.

"Smoke, Rogue."

"Wait, Rogue?" Daemon asked. "He was in a Stark suit."

And not even just a Stark suit. They'd boosted the suit months ago from the armoire of an Enterprise notable who'd turned up dead the next day. Nobody wanted those things floating around. Now they'd left one behind, and with all of Daemon's modifications. Two people, one massive piece of equipment — gone.

As clusterfucks went, the robbery was starting to look like at least six out of ten.

"Conventional rounds," Ryu told him.

"I lined it with Kevlar!"

"He took it out. Said it was too restrictive. His exact words were, 'It's a goddamn Stark suit. It's its own armor.'"

Chase laughed again. Smoke's death, at least, should have been news to Chase because even Savage hadn't seen her die. Chase had been trying to scoop Rogue from that goddamn robot suit at the time like meat from a lobster's shell, knowing it was futile and he was merely making their escape harder. Yet this was his response to a teammate's death: *laughter*.

Savage would definitely be teaching him some manners once the dust finally settled.

"You think it's funny?" Locus demanded.

He had disobeyed a prime directive and spent many loud hours banging Smoke in the pod's equipment locker. Maybe it was supposed to be a secret but Ryu let it fly and now Chase was about to have his head knocked off for abject insensitivity.

"I wasn't laughing about Smoke," Chase told him.

"Rogue, then?" Twilight asked. "If you were going to be a prick, why'd you try to save him?"

"I guess I'm not a prick, then." Chase moved closer to Twilight. "I guess I'm sensitive. This is my coping mechanism." He put a hand on the wall just over Twilight's shoulder. He wasn't attracted to her, but he was well aware of how much he repulsed her, so the taunt wasn't at all unexpected. "You know what other way I like to cope?"

Ryu looked around. He'd designed the pod himself: space-saving tech that employed holography and subtle omnidirectional treadmills underfoot to make a small place feel twice its actual size, and perceptual tricks to fool the senses.

"Where's Nero? Is he in the bunk room?"

Savage shook her head. "Nero didn't make it."

"He's dead?"

"Sorry. He didn't make it to the punch-out point. I suppose he could still be out there."

Ryu looked around at the others, then at his watch. He wore one; they were on total and complete Beam blackout unless the network was accessed through his anonymizer. He had made that himself, too — his solution to the problem of The Beam's intelligence.

You couldn't just scramble information sent to The Beam, because the AI recorded everything and had an infinity of time to untangle even the toughest encryption if it cared to do so. The odds of spoofed or encrypted traffic ever coming back to bite them was remote in the absolute worst-case scenario, but Ryu was paranoid to a degree Savage had never seen before.

Instead of scrambling messages, Ryu's add-on sent them faithfully using what he called "drunk Beam-like agents." He'd basically created his own Beam-compatible agents, then used a process Savage didn't want to know about to essentially drive them insane. They'd do the job without revealing the source, seeing as they no longer had that capacity.

"How much time?" Locus was hating the blackout. Without Beam connectivity, his specs were merely somewhat intelligent sunglasses. He could see a lot of stuff the others couldn't, but it was a lot like having a doctor on call who could tell you exactly how sick you were without being anywhere close to a cure.

"Two minutes."

"I keep telling you," Chase said, "it's time to fly."

"Two minutes," Ryu repeated.

"Please. I saw Nero hit. They got him in the side."

"Where in the side?"

"The fuck's it matter where?" Chase answered. "He's gonna slow down, they're gonna pinch him, and then they'll get him talking."

"He won't talk." Ryu shook his head. "We have contingencies."

"Like you had a Stark suit?"

Now Ryu looked angry. He had face-length black hair and an even darker beard on a long, hawk-like face. "I saw you talking to Rogue about the Kevlar."

"What, you think I talked him out of it?"

"Someone did. Because I sure as hell made it clear that—"

"You think something else you're not saying, Ryu?"

His eyes grew hard. Ryu was wearing dark glasses, but Savage was close enough to see through them. She had a good idea what he was thinking.

They'd been double-crossed. The plan was airtight enough (in her mind, anyway, and she'd looked and looked) that this level of failure shouldn't have been possible without a leak.

Ryu was an artist. He'd designed a heist strategy that was perfect by way of its imperfections. Every possible disaster was considered and solved-for, its many parts made modular and redundant. Anything that went bad was supposed to be severable like a gangrenous limb: triage to keep failure from spreading.

What they'd found inside Xenia Labs had undone most of that, and idiocy like Rogue removing the Kevlar from their primary weapon or Chase trying to drag him out dead finished off the job. They hadn't counted on private security using ammo illegal enough to shut all of Xenia down. Even so, the Kevlar would have plugged the suit joints that were impervious to energy weapons yet plenty vulnerable to a perfectly aimed bullet.

Not that aim had been necessary. At least two of the black-jacketed combatants above were carrying BBR5s — a weapon with a conventional-slug RPM the world hadn't seen since the MAC-10 or Uzi. Fire that much lead in one direction and eventually you'll get lucky. Or unlucky, in Rogue's case.

Savage thought Ryu might outright accuse Chase, but adrenaline and tempers were high, their collective fear compressed into knots of aggression like pressure makes coal into diamonds, with zero proof beyond instinct that they'd been ratted out or that Chase was the leak in the event that they had.

This morning, they'd been friends — or as much as

self-interested criminals could be thought of as such. The mission, though it meant different things to each of them, was the glue binding them together. They might be criminals in the eyes of NAU law, but nobody saw it that way. The job paid, yes, but only because it *had* to. None of them could take normal gigs without risking exposure. More important than money (to most of them, Savage believed) was the ideal that Ryu had presented for them.

What if there was no more Beau Monde? And what if what Xenia actually had was available to everyone?

Ryu wasn't exactly kumbaya and didn't believe the world's problems would simply disappear once the tech gap was eliminated, but he hated the way everyone was forced to play a rigged game.

Choose Option A or Choose Option B, the parties said — *Enterprise or Directorate, you choose your fate!*

But really Option A and Option B were the same thing, and both lived under the heel of Option C, which nobody was permitted to see, let alone aspire to.

You were born Beau Monde or you were pulled up and into it by back-scratching buddies, but it couldn't be earned. It was a club with its doors locked. Implying freedom in a world of lies was even more insulting than unfair. And that was Ryu's reason for this, Savage believed. He didn't want technological equality so much as he hated having his intelligence insulted. The mission meant as much to him as it did to her. She trusted him more than she trusted just about anyone else in the world, and had quietly given Ryu a ring to show they were friends and not just co-conspirators in this impossible heist.

Ryu shook his head and turned away.

Chase took this as a victory. "Let's talk about you, then."

He followed Ryu across the pod. The treadmills underfoot grew confused, interpreting his walk-off as him wanting to get away, but then interpreting Chase's pursuit as something Ryu might not have noticed.

Ryu walked faster but Chase easily caught him.

"Conventional ammo," he said to Ryu's profile. "Noah Fucking West, Ryu — you wanna tell me why the fuck they were firing conventional ammo?"

"It was on sale."

"Is this a joke to you?" Chase grabbed him by the shoulder of his leather jacket, then immediately realized he'd made a mistake.

He let go, but not before Ryu gave him a death stare.

"Look," Chase continued. "I'm not saying it's your fault. But it's for goddamn sure *someone's*."

"You could have worn Kevlar, if you were so worried." Asp wore an eyepatch. It was in no way necessary, because even if he couldn't afford a replacement eye (he absolutely could), Ryu had boxes of spares. They weren't as fancy as Savage's, but they'd at least fill the hole in his face and give him some depth perception. His hair was unruly and long and reminded Savage of a lion's mane. His words were all snarls. Savage had never felt threatened by someone saying *Hello* before meeting Asp.

Chase said, "Look who's talking."

"I got shot in the leg, asswipe. Your buddy was a target. He thought the extra weight wasn't worth it? Obviously he'd be the first one shot."

"*If* we'd known they'd be shooting lead."

"*We're* shooting lead."

"We're the goddamn bad guys! Of course we're shooting lead! They're—"

"We're not the bad guys." Daemon was putting two old-fashioned circuit boards together in a fashion so clumsy, it looked like a little girl bumping dolls to pretend they were kissing.

Of course, he wasn't actually clumsy, though his white-haired-old-man look sure made it seem that way. Daemon's work with those two old boards would've probably won him a Nobel Prize in the pre-Renewal days.

"You know what I mean," Chase said.

Tenor nodded. "We're bad to the bone, baby."

"I just think we need to stop talking like that. Words have meaning. If you think you're—"

"Time," Ryu called.

"Thank West."

Asp looked at Chase. "Pretty eager to leave a teammate behind, aren't you?"

"If he's dead, yes. If he's pinched, yes."

"What if he just got his balls shot off, like you?"

"I didn't get …" Chase stopped and scowled.

Asp smiled. *Bullseye.*

"Spool up," Ryu said. "Twilight, cover Nero's spot."

"What about the others' spots?" Asp asked.

"No problem. I'll take Rogue's and you take Smoke's." Tenor grabbed a bag of potato chips from the cabinet and flopped on the couch, then he pointed between Asp and Locus. "You've sucked his dick before, right?"

Asp made to stand, wincing as he rolled over his injured leg. Tenor laughed again. Savage, as she sat back and let the appointed people handle departure, went about the task of hating Tenor even more than she already did.

Maybe humor really was his defense mechanism, but if so, Savage wanted to give him a lot more to defend against. Adrenaline and fear aside, two of their number died today. Smoke and Rogue had had friends, even families. It wasn't funny in the least and she intended to prove it once given a chance.

"Belts on," Ryu said. Then, after a pause: *"Jump."*

Savage had never gotten used to the sensation of a pod jump. It wasn't actually a jump, for one. The action was closer to diving, or drilling, while being precisely neither of those things. Digging was concussive; anything from the earthquake folks to amateur geeks with their ears on the ground could sense it and, if they wished, follow.

The pod did something closer to an earthbound breast-stroke, using electrostatic tech like that in the ocean levies to soundlessly push even hard-packed ground aside molecule by molecule, then nanobots like those in the NAU dome to hold the works back with a carbon nanotube mesh. The works was broken down as the pod passed.

More of Ryu's tech — stuff Xenia could have developed if they weren't so preoccupied with making rich people perfect, before turning them immortal.

On the jump command, the pre-energized ground atomized fast enough that the sensation was that of an old-fashioned elevator with its counterweights cut. Savage always felt like she was going to barf.

When they'd reach depth and were moving fluidly to the backup rendezvous point (good luck, Nero — you're gonna need it), Savage saw Locus, bored, begin to toe the backpack he'd been wearing on the job. He'd set it aside in all the blood and commotion — a funny thing, considering how important it was. Officially, two people (so far) had given their lives to fill that backpack and one had been wounded. Nero might be among its victims, too; they'd have to wait and see.

Savage moved to sit by Locus. They'd be down here a while, moving fairly fast but with a long way to go.

He considered her but said nothing. Locus wasn't afraid of her, and that was nice. She looked a little like beef jerky even on her best days, and some genetic trick made her eye sockets deep, shadows giving them what looked like permanent black eyes. After growing tired of being asked if someone had beaten her up, Savage finally leaned into her image. Now she let people assume her not-actually-black eyes were collateral damage from a fight in which she'd doled out much worse.

"Okay, Savage?"

"Okay, Locus. You?"

"Not good. Smoke …"

"I know." She gave him a look, but that was all the sympathy he'd get. They were professionals. Nobody expected sappy displays even at the worst times. Everyone here had signed up knowing full well that there might be casualties. Smoke had just drawn one of the short straws.

"You got it," she said of the backpack.

It wasn't empty. She'd thought it would be, because the original contents were jettisoned by necessity and she'd assumed there was no time to fill it with dreams during their little melee. Shit had gone so bad so fast, a part of her brain had forgotten they'd gone to Xenia with a goal.

"Sort of. Maybe."

A strange answer. They'd been looking for a code nexus, and the existence of that nexus wasn't a *sort of, maybe* thing. Back in the days of Crossbrace, it was still possible to undo encryption with brute force (even though doing so took ages) because that network had been built by humans.

The Beam, on the other hand, had been built by the AI that evolved inside Crossbrace. It stopped being under-standable by human minds around the time Noah West had died, and even back then he was the only person who came close to understanding.

Beam codes couldn't be cracked by humans alone. AI assistance was always required. Even back then the AIs had to know the other AIs who'd birthed the code in the first place. And that's what Ryu's group had been after: Xenia's heavily firewalled codemaking AI, from which Ryu believed he could clone codebreakers.

And impossible as that might have seemed to anyone on the outside, Savage believed it. Ryu's tech was better than Xenia's because he worked in Little Harajuku within District Zero, where innovation was driven by necessity. By contrast, Xenia was fueled by profit and could only move so fast. Unfortunately, they also had a lock on the upgrades sector, encoding the protocols that let their add-ons work with The Beam, thus effectively sidelining all competing tech. *Censored*, really.

It wasn't that Xenia had all the upgrades wisdom in the modern North American Union; it was that they'd throttled all knowledge that didn't come from Xenia.

Xenia sold the best of that knowledge to the upper one percent — the so-called Beau Monde class — and erased its tracks so the lower ninety-nine didn't know those premium upgrades even existed. Without that artificial information blockade, the NAU would be a very different place. Hence Ryu's plan to upend Xenia's cookie jar. And hence the code nexus, which would make it all possible.

The thing was, Ryu's intel said the nexus was actually simple. The AIs that comprised it were small enough to fit on a plain-old slip drive. Ryu had taken his drives and cables just to be sure (or in case they found other salacious Xenia data ripe for the copying) but she'd watched the pack unzipped in preparation, then dumped empty in the surprise of the first ambush.

If the pack was full now, it could only contain something new. But why was that something-new so big? Savage had assumed, when asking Locus if he'd gotten the nexus, that the device had been bigger than expected — maybe they'd had to yank and steal an entire set of drives instead of delicately copying information to a slip. But his reply suggested that wasn't the case.

Sort of. Maybe. It was stranger than *I don't know.* That answer implied they'd gotten something but hadn't had a chance yet to see if it contained the code nexus they'd been looking for.

Sort of and *maybe* both said something else.

Something less defined.

Something out of the ordinary.

"What do you mean?"

"It wasn't the way Ryu said," Locus told her.

"No shit." Savage looked at Asp.

The fact that only one of the remaining eight (maybe nine) had been wounded was downright miraculous. Only after they'd gotten out had Savage allowed herself to breathe, wondering *how* and *why* they managed to get out. The forces they'd met had been perfectly prepared to thwart them and hadn't seemed at all surprised. It was like they'd been waiting.

Ryu seemed to believe that they'd been ratted out. But if that was true, then why were any of them still breathing? Savage swore she'd seen armed soldiers hold the others back not once but three separate times. It was enough to make her feel toyed with.

"No," Locus said. "I don't mean the job. I mean the clean room."

Savage wanted to shake her head. A clean room was a clean room was a clean room. Small technicians wore neutral white jumpsuits and rubber-soled shoes, building circuits that didn't dictate the way devices worked anymore so much as gave sentient data options for where to play. Clean rooms had dry benches, halon fire suppression systems, shielded terminals, and *many* carefully managed parts.

The clean room should have harbored zero surprises.

"Did you have trouble getting inside?"

Locus shook his head. His blacked-out specs made it look like his eyes were blank, or missing.

"Different upgrades inside?" Savage guessed. "Apparently they moved all the Series Six nanobots to a room on the other side of—"

Locus stopped her with a head-shake so subtle, she might have imagined it.

"What, then?"

"There was no clean room."

But that was like saying there was no sun in the sky.

At first, she didn't understand. The plan had clearly gone tits-up. They'd found unregistered private security firing illegal rounds; that security had seemed to follow them in (without engaging) and then out (after engaging); despite Tenor's quip about DZPD, they'd not seen a single cop — even after their thunderous exit from the building, a gunfight on the streets of District Zero, and getting spotted by enough civilians for The Beam to sic a hundred auto-cops on them before they could flee the core network.

But ... *no clean room?*

That was the one thing Ryu had been *certain* about. They'd all watched his nanocam footage, seeing the heist's layout with their own eyes. The recovery crew was to enter the lobby, head left, then hold the employees at bay while they copied what they needed. That entire side of the building was a clean room.

Wrong clean room would have made more sense than *no* clean room.

"What?" Savage said. "How could there be no clean room?"

Locus removed his specs. "See for yourself."

His eyes were too normal beneath them. She expected empty pits, every time.

She donned his specs, then keyed a time index a few minutes into the heist. She observed the scene from his point of view as he led the charge, watched data gates open doors with his enhanced vision. So far, the mission seemed to be unfolding as expected. Savage didn't understand all of Ryu's models, but she understood enough to know they were working.

Everything was as predicted until she heard the guns going off — auditory input that on Locus would be funneled straight through his implants and into his brain.

The first shots fired had been aimed at Rogue — at the seam in his armored Stark suit, seeming to know he wore no Kevlar, as if they understood the need to disarm his suit first and drastically limit the intruders' options.

The unexpected guards had known just where to hit the suit with armor-piercing conventional bullets, bringing it down and killing its occupant.

Rogue had never stood a chance.

Following the shots, people in Locus's group began shouting commands. Mainly Ryu, saying, "Go go go!"

They burst through the final door, all of them surely expecting to see the same thing. In the pre-heist intel — taken just one day earlier — there'd been a massive clean room through that last door. But in the footage Savage was seeing now, the room was entirely empty. It looked almost sealed, as if sprayed with matte Plasteel. The echoes, from what she could hear, were all wrong. His readouts went blank, too, as if the room was a giant Faraday cage.

The room had only one door. No people, windows, equipment, or lighting fixtures — illumination seemed to come from the walls themselves. No electromagnetic signals, no in-room transmissions, no subvocal AI chatter like the kind her augmented ears sometimes picked up.

The space was entirely dead, all corners rounded just enough to muffle echoes and make the space look and sound like the near vacuum it was.

A lone object sat on the floor in the room's exact center. A charcoal-gray box, painted as matte as the walls, ceiling, and floor. A perfect cube, a dozen or so inches per side.

She handed the specs back to Locus, her world now upended. It felt like they'd broken into the wrong building. The wrong company. The wrong city, the wrong continent. That didn't look like Xenia labs, and it sure as hell wasn't a console with a code nexus on it, copied to a boring old slip drive.

As Locus put his specs back on, Savage found herself looking at the backpack with a sinking feeling. She needed to open it but suddenly didn't want to.

She looked at him and he nodded. Then she made herself undo it.

Inside was the box. Cold to the touch, heavier than she'd expected, and entirely featureless. No screen, buttons, or ports. It might as well have been a shaped piece of granite, an end cap for a luxury countertop.

"What the hell …" Savage started to say.

But then the pod suddenly stopped moving. It shuddered as the atomized, charged rock cloud ahead of and behind them froze in place.

It was a chilling sensation, being locked in solid ground. Savage wondered if they'd suffocate down here, deep enough that it'd take a sounding to find them. Nobody but Ryu knew his tech and few would understand it. Archaeologists finding the pod a week later would swear they'd been buried for millions of years, because how else would they have gotten there without disturbing the earth around them?

Ryu was clicking furiously through controls, seemingly at a loss. The others were all up and chattering. Everyone knew this wasn't a normal stall-out. Something had gone terribly wrong.

But Savage couldn't stop looking at the box in her hands. A display had come alight, looking almost like it had been etched into the surface with a fiery pen.

At the top of the display, it read, *ITERATION 2 OF 11*.

Below that, an in-progress timer that seemed to have been counting down for six hours, thirty-two minutes, and forty-five seconds exactly.

There were fifteen seconds left.

Then fourteen.

Then thirteen.

Chapter Three

ASP

Twelve seconds.

Eleven.

Asp saw a rare opportunity. So often in life, chances to say something cool were wasted because the right line couldn't be thought of fast enough. And that didn't count those times when there was mortal peril to consider.

Movies had it easier. As a turn-of-the-millennium movie buff, few people knew that better than Asp. John McClane hadn't needed to think before saying (twice, and both at super-cool times) "Yippie-ki-yay, motherfucker!" to Hans Gruber. That badass line had been in the script. John never would have spit something so great if he'd been a real guy in a genuine moment.

Asp was easily as badass as John McClane. Everyone said so, even if they never mentioned Mr. McClane specifically, on account of most people having no idea who he was. Asp usually got a blanket benediction for his coolness, irrespective of certain old movie stars. The eyepatch helped. And he did try for one-liners, when opportunities arose.

In the middle of a robbery, in the outer districts where nanobot and hover penetration was minimal and he could still get away with such things, he was accused of not having the guts to shoot those who disobeyed.

Asp looked that man in his eyes and said, "Count to ten and let's find out."

It didn't mean much, but it was pretty sweet in retrospect. Another time, when a negotiation went bad, he found himself on one side of a two-man standoff. His opponent looked like he couldn't handle the pressure. So Asp said, "Your move, creep."

Technically, that was Robocop's line, but the philistines today had no idea. Asp considered shouting "Yippie-ki-yay, motherfucker!" as the guy ran off, but he didn't want to press his luck. You could only steal lines from big films for so long.

He thought fast. Asp was lying back because of his injury, shot leg up until they could find a dermal kit. The position also made it look like everyone was freaking out while he was too cool to give a shit, so he removed one of the strike-anywhere matches from his boot and struck one on his sole.

He plucked a cigarette (mimicked, of course — who could afford real tobacco before their heist paid off?) from an inner pocket and spoke in a gravel-filled voice.

"If I'm goin' out, I'm goin' out smok—"

"IT'S A BOMB!"

That was Tenor, not being cool at all and rudely shouting over the best line in the room. How gauche. Asp had looked over; he'd seen the box with the readout on its upside and the faces of the two people who'd spied the countdown first. He was no dummy. He could put two and two together, and every early action movie from *Goldfinger* to *Executive Decision* knew that when something in the shape of a rectangle counted down to zero, a big BOOM was coming.

They were currently buried in rock with seconds to go. What exactly was there to do? Asp didn't plan to spend his final few seconds of life being a pussy, but Tenor had apparently decided otherwise.

He pulled out the rest of his cigarettes. Not like he'd need them after this. So in a rare twofer, Asp came up with a second thing to say.

"Any'a the resta you wanna die like—?"

Locus pushed past him in what was probably an attempt to flee the box.

Savage dropped it a microsecond later, then tromped by, same as Locus.

Locus knocked Asp to the floor and Savage stepped on his hand.

This was not a good way to go.

The box had fallen on its side. The readout was visible to everyone in the pod. Asp took the final second to wonder if it would liquify them (with rock to their backs, it seemed possible if not probable), then tried to live his last blip of life like Leon, The Professional.

Tick.

The box went dark. Nothing happened.

Except that Chase, Asp was pretty sure, had just pissed his charming foreigner's pants. The pod suddenly smelled of urine. Chase turned one-eighty, trying to seem nonchalant while looking for something to cover his soiled front.

"Well. That was fun," Asp said, lighting his cigarette again.

The cherry was already glowing, but he wanted to strike a match on his boot while everyone wasn't occupied with their eyes on something else.

A hum began in the pod's belly. Lights he hadn't

noticed dimming returned to full brightness. There was a shudder and a lurch, then the works began to move.

The pod was tunneling again, all systems seemingly back to normal.

"We're green." Ryu's voice was even, but he blinked just enough for Asp to see his fear. Even Asp had been frightened. Maybe. Just a tiny little bit. "We're moving again."

"What happened?" Locus asked.

"I don't know."

"Did it have anything to do with the box?"

"What box?" Daemon had donned goggles that looked a lot like Locus's, but they were inert, not Beam-enabled at all.

Asp had seen Daemon using them for welding in the past, but now maybe the old man was simply going for weird. Asp had no plans to be strange when he aged like Daemon. He'd either die young(ish) in a blaze of glory, use his heist take to buy age-stopping nanobot treatment and look his action hero best forever, or get old and grizzled for good, like Sam Elliott or Kris Kristofferson.

Daemon didn't appear to be kidding. He hadn't noticed the box in their scant few seconds of warning. A few of the others had, but most reacted to Tenor's bellow, coming so soon after the weird pod shutdown.

Now a few of them were looking at Tenor.

"I guess it's not a bomb," he said.

Asp righted himself, pulling his butt along the deck until he was beside the box. Savage had abandoned the thing, and Locus was the only one looking its way. He looked more responsible than interested. The backpack was open beside it. Locus seemed to think someone should put the box back inside … but ideally not him.

Asp picked it up.

Locus looked away, the buck now passed.

Daemon sat beside him, his voice like a human saw.

"What is it?" The old man's hands went out, waiting for the box.

Asp, who had to admit that the thing creeped him right the hell out, handed the box right over. Ryu was their pirate technologist, but Daemon was the mad scientist. Ryu might try to get the thing working — *whatever* it did — but Daemon was their best bet to understand its *whats* and *hows*.

Daemon had been an orphan because he wouldn't stop taking his family's canvas apart, and that had been in the early days, probably pre-Beam, when Crossbrace terminals weren't even called canvases yet. His parents, who'd been deeply tech-addicted like most of the NAU back then (and today, though nobody called it that), had chosen a functional system over their son.

Daemon had gone to foster homes and halfway houses after that, but he disassembled everything there as well. He aged out eventually, moved into the corpse of an early Quark network prototype, and lived like a homeless man with a genius IQ. He owned more underground patents than Asp's tallied birthdays, but it was all black-market money. Daemon didn't care. Give him a gadget to strip and he'd be giddy in the holding tank of a public toilet.

But Daemon didn't immediately try to open it. There were no screws, pressure hatches, or obvious magnetic seams. The box felt like a block of polished rock, more like Xenia's top-secret paperweight than anything they could use.

Asp began to second-guess his assumption. He'd been thinking of his post-heist life and all the money he'd soon be enjoying ... but the pinch hadn't exactly gone according to plan. They hadn't recovered the code nexus, so they couldn't crack open the vaults and spill Xenia's best-kept secrets.

Their plan suggested the crew could be altruists *and* capitalists. Xenia's covert tech — the kind they sold only to one percent of the one-percenters — would soon be pirated on every street corner. The poor and disenfranchised would win because they'd suddenly be tech-peers with the so-called Beau Monde. And the sellers of that tech would become the new Xenias, albeit without all the inequality.

Asp and his crew would be rich. Pirate tech would spawn copycat pirate tech, and soon there'd be no more secrets. Everyone would win. Except for the powerful, who would be slightly less powerful, and Xenia, who would be very much out of business.

Asp was fine with those casualties.

But this box? It wasn't what they'd gone to Xenia Labs to steal. He'd been right there when Locus opened the door to what should have been a clean room, and he'd been just as *what the fuck?* as the rest of the retrieval party.

The box had creeped him out then, and it creeped him out now.

Who would want to buy *this* thing?

"Interesting," Daemon said.

"What's interesting?"

"There's a ridiculous amount of data streaming in and out of this thing. A *ridiculous* amount. I've never seen anything quite like it."

"How are you seeing it now?"

"Interesting."

"Daemon?"

"So much data. It's so … intriguing …"

Asp wanted to hit him. Daemon didn't really live in the real world. He was more real-world adjacent. He knew the language, but few of its customs. Talking to Daemon was like having a conversation with a robot that had been programmed to do only one task to the exclusion of everything else. Something Asp had no use for. Folding tortillas, perhaps, or playing immersive checkers.

"Daemon," he tried again.

The old man finally looked up with his mouth open. This was as close as he ever came to giving attention.

"Locus scoped it. There's no Fi. No ports and no wires."

"That is correct."

"No bend at all in a Beam data stream run parallel. We carried it out in a Faraday cage. *This pod* is a Faraday cage. How can it have any I/Os at all?"

"Fascinating," Daemon answered.

"Did you hear my question?"

"It has an aura. You should see it."

"Okay," said Asp, already tired of this. "Show it to me."

Daemon walked away. Asp wasn't sure if he was supposed to follow. It probably didn't matter. Daemon seldom noticed other people even if they were right around him. He could probably follow the guy into a bathroom stall while he relieved himself, and the old man would barely stop calculating.

"Watch," Daemon told Asp when they reached the area he'd co-opted as a micro workshop. He reached into one of many vials in a sagging cardboard box, pinched out something that looked like very fine gray powder, then sprinkled it in the air just above the box.

The powder did not fall to the counter or onto the box. It formed a cloud that hovered over it, revolving in a lazy swirl.

"What is that?"

"Its aura."

"What, like the nutballs talk about? The anthro-posophists? Are you talking about some bullshit like Seren-ityBlue?"

"No, no. This is real. Even in the way you talk about real." Daemon reached toward Asp without moving his eyes from the box and its odd cloud, then started snapping as if he wanted the other man to hand him a tool. "Give me your mobile."

"Ryu said no devices. Nothing connected."

"I know that." Daemon sounded annoyed, as if Asp was being obtuse on purpose. "It doesn't work, but you *have* it, right?"

Yeah. He wasn't supposed to, but Asp hadn't seen the harm. Ryu could control just about anything with a Beam pulse simply by looking in its direction, or so it sometimes seemed. He'd insisted everyone leave all Beam-connected peripherals at home unless they were inside their bodies, but even the implants were easy because nobody on the job had official add-ons sold by legitimate dealers.

All of their tech was underground, which meant Ryu could pull its strings. Beam-connected devices they could hold in their hands were another story. Mobiles, for instance. They were too easy and too cheap to buy off the shelf — something Ryu was less able to control for.

Still, they'd all neutered those devices with software before starting and Ryu carried a signal detector that would alarm (and probably get the offender shot) if anyone broke the rules. Ryu's insistence on not even bringing mobiles and tablets was just an extra layer of protection.

That layer, Asp had felt confident to break.

"Don't tell Ryu," Asp said, but Daemon never would.

He took his mobile and held it over the box, still watching something that Asp couldn't imagine. Daemon didn't have enhanced eyes, so this was surely something else.

If he really meant *aura*, he'd be using his Ayurvedic third eye or some other hippie bullshit, but Asp didn't think the translation was that simple. What Daemon did with circuits and data matrices was more like magic to most of them — but it worked, so they'd all quit asking questions.

"Want me to unlock it?" Asp asked.

"No."

"Because it's locked."

"I don't want you to unlock it," Daemon told him.

"I mean locked with an AI."

"I know what you mean. Be quiet."

Asp kept wanting to interject. Normal mobiles locked on a whole host of biometric or Beam-handshake cues that were impossible to break even with Ryu's tech. That wasn't a coincidence. To say that their de facto leader didn't trust easily was an understatement.

Ryu famously gave an interview to that author guy, Sterling something-or-other, for his book about The Beam — *Plugged*. The reporter was blinded with a very special bag over his head, sense-neutered, relocated, and ended up talking to Ryu in what must have felt like a warlord situation. It was six months into planning this job before Asp even got to meet him, and the trials he'd had to surmount for the privilege nearly made him bail. Only Twilight's vouching kept him interested. She promised that if Asp declined an invite from Ryu, he'd end up regretting it without a doubt, and likely for the rest of his life.

But that paranoia went two ways, so Asp had visited not one but four of Ryu's competitors before joining the crew, presenting *keeping Ryu out of my shit* as a challenge they might not be hacker enough to follow through on. He'd found himself with a mobile that annoyed even Asp to unlock.

"Ah," said Daemon, nodding. "Your penis."

Asp sat upright fast enough to wrench his wound painfully. He spied his mobile's screen, now unlocked and displaying a photo he'd sent to someone who very much hadn't wanted it three or four years back. The pic had been erased long ago. Deleted once and then again from the trash, the works formatted twice since as he'd upgraded and remapped his settings.

"What the fuck?" Asp snatched the mobile back.

His four-layer code-and-biometric locks weren't just open; they seemed to be gone entirely. The mobile appeared to be rooted, one swipe away from terminal access that wasn't accessible outside of the factory where the things were built. His OS was still there, but he had to engage the thing.

It was as if everything in the thing had been asked to get naked, then responded with gusto.

He swiped through the menus with uneasy fascination. Asp had plunged pretty deep into his mobile's code, but there were things in here that he'd never seen. Everything he'd ever erased was now available, not just that one photo.

Asp pocketed the mobile before he could think too much about it. "What is that thing, Daemon?"

"It's a codebreaker, but nothing like the one we expected to find."

Chapter Four

TENOR

"Look," Daemon said.

He was being lucid — almost like a normal person. That happened so rarely, it became an occasion when he did. Without Daemon, the mission wouldn't have been possible, but even with the whacky old fucker, there weren't usually many chances to find out why.

Tenor thought Daemon was probably a savant of some sort, but "crazy" was an easier term. And he didn't think there was anything wrong with using it, since people called him crazy, too.

The pod was stopped, intentionally this time. They'd been floating in a haze of atomized rock for long enough now that Tenor wished they'd surface for some fresh air. Ryu's tunnel voodoo was impressive but terrifying.

What if Ryu had a heart attack? Nobody else would have a clue what to do. Ryu showed him — and everyone else — why they had to stay down here a while. The pod had a periscope function, but it was probably just a signal that hijacked stray hoverbots topside and formed them into a mechanical cornea behind a rudimentary lens.

He could show them what was happening directly above. They appeared to be below a bombed-out section of rural New York state, meaning they'd tunneled under the Hudson. There was a two-hundred-year-old barn on one side of the screen and a magnetosphere-driven windmill on the other. Windmills like that cost more than a District Zero apartment. Were these farmers growing opium?

A hovering black ship the size of a Wild East ocean liner occupied the center of that image. There were no markings, but that didn't matter. Tenor didn't need written instructions to know they'd best not meet the occupants of that ship.

"They followed us," Chase said when he saw it. "We didn't get away clean."

Then he seemed to decide it was Asp's fault, perhaps because Asp had been injured. The logic was specious even for Tenor.

"No." Ryu pulled up a string of logs and pointed as if conclusions drawn from them might be visible for anyone else. "They showed up six minutes ago. And there's something else. Look."

The view changed, now a map instead of a camera view, with a pair of dots that were nearly close enough to overlap, a line that looped back on itself once behind one of them.

"This line is our path. It looks like this because when we came out this far" — Ryu touched the far edge of the loop — "I decided to go back."

"Why?" Twilight was holding the massive gun she'd used for the heist, probably to make herself seem tougher.

"Because I saw the ship."

"You went *back* to find the ship? But if you think it's—"

Ryu nodded, causing his long black hair to swing like

curtains in front of his face. "I do think it's them." He didn't bother to say who *them* referred to because everyone already knew. "But the ship didn't follow us."

"I don't get what you're saying," Chase told him.

"This is the moment when the black ship showed up." Ryu rolled back the onscreen time index. Seeing the result, the people around the table became much more interested. The two dots were on top of each other, but their pod hadn't yet made the double-back loop. "It appeared directly above us, then stayed where it was without following. I thought we should go back to investigate."

"How long ago was this?" Savage asked.

Ryu nodded at her as if she'd solved a problem presented by no one. "Six minutes ago." He glanced at his watch. "Almost seven, now."

"What?" Tenor asked again.

"That's when the box hit zero," Ryu explained. "The pod went dead and that thing appeared above us."

"You saying they're related?"

"I'm saying it's an awfully big coincidence."

Conversation spiraled for several minutes. Twilight suggested they never surface, at least not until they figured this out, but Ryu shook his head.

"Tunneling takes a lot of power. Rods are tracked, so for something like this I use AluBatteries." He tapped a section of the screen, showing a graphic dial with its needle all the way to the left. "The charge won't last forever. I planned to jump us to the backup rendezvous."

"Fuck the rendezvous," Chase said. "Nero's dead."

"It's not just about Nero. I have a charging array there. We come up anywhere else, we'll be stuck there."

More conversation. More hypotheses.

This was the first time most of the group was seeing

the box, realizing only now that they'd planned an entire heist that hadn't happened.

Locus showed a mission record captured on his specs, and it creeped Tenor right the fuck out. He'd already started thinking they had to have been betrayed — probably by someone on the inside — but the footage practically confirmed it.

Xenia had reconfigured their entire operation and stocked it with fresh guards within twenty-four hours of their arrival. Another healthy-sized coincidence.

But if Xenia knew they were coming, why did they leave the box in the room? Why was the room itself so different? Just how the hell had they gotten away, through all those expectant guns?

Even Ryu couldn't explain the box. They'd been underway again for a half hour by the time Daemon revealed his discovery, Ryu having delegated piloting the pod to Savage so they could resume progress to the checkpoint before the batteries ran dry. Ryu himself disappeared with Daemon, the two of them retreating to a small outer-ring lab while everyone else was told to sit tight and behave, as if they were a bunch of kindergarteners.

That irked Tenor. Enough to do something about it. He'd gotten into this for the payday, and didn't particularly feel like embarking upon a science experiment with some weird little box. They were supposed to be in and out of Xenia, which they had, and emerge with something immediately salable, which they hadn't.

The black box felt like fathoms deep tech to Tenor, and that made him acutely uneasy. It unlocked coded secrets like the flipping of a switch, which made him feel naked. He began giving the box a wide berth, afraid it wouldn't just unlock the shielded relay he had installed before the job but would actually reach through it and start shouting about Tenor's little side deal.

Simply put, he didn't trust Ryu, or like him holding all the cards. So he'd taken out some insurance, with extra profit as a side effect. Not a good thing for his fellow rebels to discover — especially not Savage, who might as well be rimming Ryu for all the altruism she'd been pouring into her role.

The two of them seemed to think they were Robin Hood, rather than a pair of common thieves. Tenor was just more honest than they were.

So he found Locus. Locus had a beef with Ryu and Chase over the thing with Smoke, but that beef had all been Smoke's fault. Tenor had seen the way she grabbed her ear during the job, as if getting a call on one of her wetchips.

Their chips were dampened and encoded, so how was Smoke still getting calls?

She had hacked through Ryu's doings somehow, maybe pulling a double-cross like the one Tenor had been planning.

She got shot. She broke through Ryu's cypher and broke Beam silence. That had gotten her killed. So what?

Locus was level-headed enough to get that, even if he'd been fucking her.

"Locus, listen." Tenor pulled the big man aside, knowing he'd have to talk fast and make his case or Locus would likely rip the skin from his body. "I found something. I've been looking through the pod vitals from when everything stopped."

"Why?"

"Because Ryu's keeping something from us. I think it got Smoke killed."

That was a stretch. In truth, what he'd found had

nothing to do with Smoke, so that meant Tenor would have to do some fast-talking. He was good at that.

But it was also a stretch to say he'd found something and that he'd been looking through the pod vitals. In reality, he'd turned on a panel to see if there was anything on the pod juke to take his mind off all this boredom, and the thing he claimed to have "found" was right there. The box must have decoded it while screwing up operations — and, it seemed, calling the black ship above through unknown means.

What Tenor found — and what he showed Locus with a lot of leading language and questionable conclusions — was a log showing excess power consumption coming from the pod's batteries. The extra power was going to a data array near the pod's atomizing engines. He thought it looked like an antenna.

Tenor suspected Ryu was double-dealing all along; that's why he'd started doing the same thing. To protect himself.

Locus asked what this had to do with Smoke's death.

Tenor explained that if Ryu's probably-an-antenna was sending info about their mission to someone else, he was obviously the mole in their midst — the traitor who'd informed Xenia that they were coming and ultimately ended up getting her killed. Locus was big and dumb. If Tenor made his accusations with confidence, the big galoot would likely believe it. And did.

"So what do we do? Confront him?"

Tenor didn't think so. For now, they had the advantage. The information he'd found onscreen had practically fallen into his lap. He assumed this was the codebreaker's doing. The box had cracked Asp's mobile with zero effort, and he needed only to wave the mobile in its airspace.

The box must have also decoded Ryu's scheme. Lucky

Tenor was the one to see it first, then hide that truth from the others. He was increasingly suspicious of Ryu. He'd imagined their leader with a hidden antenna, broadcasting mission data to someone else. His uncovering evidence of exactly that meant two things were true.

First, Tenor had gotten lucky. The box had let the right man find the data, seeing as anyone else would have made excuses for Ryu and assumed it was nothing.

Second, he was a genius. His blue-sky intuition had landed a bullseye.

Tenor looked to the closed door to Daemon's second workspace. "No. He's occupied playing Pat-a-Cake with Daemon, probably planning more stuff against us. Why else wouldn't they look the box over out here?"

Locus nodded. *Dummy.*

"So I say we go back to the atomizer engines. Find the array. Then we'll have proof."

"We have proof right now, don't we?"

No, he didn't. Not really. Tenor had confusing data and suspicions. He was pretty sure — no, no; he was *absolutely* sure — that Ryu was up to no good, but more of that belief relied on his genius mind than hard proof.

Anyone but Locus would have pointed that out, but then again that's why Tenor had chosen the freaky-eyed fuck as an accomplice.

"Well, yes," Tenor said. "But more proof is better."

They went to where the array seemed to be hidden, then to the weapons locker after finding nothing. Tenor pointed to an AI cloud stream he didn't remotely understand. "See! Proof!"

Locus didn't ask. He simply got outraged.

They'd brought conventional firearms for the job, but of course that liar Ryu had taken them back and stashed their cache as soon as everyone but the dead and Nero returned to the pod, stowing them in the weapons locker and then locking it down with what Ryu *claimed* was a time-and-GPS lock that wouldn't even open for him before they reached the backup rendezvous.

That was probably another lie. Fortunately, they found the weapons locker open. But there were only two guns. The rest were secured. The time lock showed that Tenor's weapon, coded to work only in his hands, had unlocked first. Then Locus's a while later.

The serendipity kept right on going. Today, everything was coming up Tenor.

"So we kill him," Locus said.

It had been absurdly easy to brainwash the guy. His mind must be locked with a toothpick or something. Locus had been in this mostly for Smoke, maybe some for the mission of social and technological equality, but now with his lover dead and the mission FUBAR, Locus seemed willing to shoot whatever might get him out of here first. Tenor had simply made the best argument to win his favor.

"Not yet." Tenor shook his head. "He's the only one who knows how to pilot the pod. We might get stuck down here if we kill him."

Locus tucked his handgun into the back of his belt. Tenor was still wearing his shoulder holster, so he filled it with his gun and donned a light jacket, zipped halfway.

They reached the rendezvous before Daemon and Ryu emerged from their lair. Locus kept looking at Tenor, raising eyebrows behind his specs, seeming to ask if they should shoot Ryu now that they'd reached the surface and begun recharging in what appeared to be another old barn.

Tenor shook his head. Daemon was holding the black box, and before anyone else died, Tenor wanted to know what they had found.

"It's a codebreaker," Ryu announced.

Tenor wanted to punch him.

"But it's nothing like any codebreaker I've ever seen. It's reprogramming the AI of anything it breaks. It's not actually having to *break* anything, really, because the reprogrammed AI just lets it in. It doesn't hack through security, nor does it need to. No matter the layers of security, it always opens the door."

"How's that possible?" Savage asked.

They'd had numerous esoteric discussions about code-making on The Beam and the nature of its cybernetic residents — discussions the rest of them were forced to endure because they shared the same pre-heist quarters. It all sounded highly complex to Tenor.

"I have no idea," Ryu told her. "Daemon either."

The wizard didn't even look over. It was like they were all talking about a third party who wasn't here.

"It's a tempest in a test tube. But here's something I do know," Ryu said.

They all leaned in.

Ryu pulled a small tablet from the backpack. "Everyone know what this is?"

Theatrical gasps made the rounds. It was a RedPanel, so named because of its bloody color.

"How did you get it?" Chase asked with his stupid accent.

"It was in the office the forward crew took midway through. There was a guy inside. He had this out, but was trying to hide it when we kicked in the door. I stuck it in my pocket, then gave it to Locus to carry in the backpack. And look."

He showed them the screen. It was rooted. All comers now had programmer access to whatever they wanted, recursive through rewritten code and supposedly zeroed sectors. Forget programmer access. This was SysOp access. *God* access.

That kind of thing couldn't be done. The devices were carried for two months before deployment by Beam Clerics — meatbags animated by sentient nanobots.

Those two months trained the devices, militarizing the AI inside them like attack dogs. Try to hack a RedPanel and they usually detonated. They couldn't be opened once synced to a given user. The things could be destroyed, but never repurposed.

"There's good news and bad news," Ryu said. "The good news is that the key goal of the mission is still on. It actually got easier and more effective. Airdrop this box onto Xenia's roof and every minimally adept user in DZ will be able to ravage their deepest archives. Forget about trying to close the tech gap, putting the lower ninety-nine on the same level as the Beau Monde. This will *obliterate* the gap, and we don't even have to wire in before we can use it. Like gaussing old magnetic media by waving an electro-magnet over it. Once we have an idea of its decoding range, we may be able to strap it to a drone and fly through windows. Anyone want to open the deep cuts of the political parties? Maybe we get this thing into Direc-torate and Enterprise headquarters and let the world see all their secrets. Hell, maybe we take it to the White House. See how long the NAU's senators stay anonymous."

Looks circled the table. It was a much bigger, much better strike than anything they'd imagined. The mission goal was to let the world see the forbidden, rich-people-only tech that Xenia had been developing for years — a haves-and-have-nots situation that had pulled the invisible strings of power for nearly all of Tenor's life.

But if Ryu was right, their win would be even better than that. Now it looked like the box was powerful enough to decode larger secrets than those from Xenia Labs. They could go after the political parties directly: Enterprise leadership, Directorate leadership … even the power of the Senate.

The identity of the senators was perhaps the NAU's most closely guarded secret, and in Ryu's oft-stated opinion, that was a giant crock of shit. People should know who was making their laws and running the land they lived in.

This boon couldn't come at a better time. Shift — the national election, which controlled the balance in the Senate — was only a few months away.

"What's the bad news?" Asp asked.

Ryu looked to Daemon, handing over the baton.

Daemon took the stage and said, "Look."

They all watched as he ran one hand along one side of the cube, then the other along the opposite side. It seemed careful, as if his movements had to be done exactly right.

There was a *click*. Laser-etched writing appeared on the up-side of the black cube. Same as they'd seen before, but its readout was slightly different:

ITERATION 2 OF 11.

And a timer, running at 5:01:52 with an elapsed duration of 1:31:08.

"Savage must have run her hands up it when she took it out of the backpack," Ryu said. "That's how you activate the display. It'll go away after a few minutes."

Asp leaned in. "Six hours and thirty-three minutes."

"Right. That's what it was the last time, only now we have another five hours until zero."

"Then what?"

"Maybe nothing. It didn't do anything the first time."

"Except call the black ship," Twilight said.

"Maybe." But Ryu didn't look sure.

"Probably." Savage looked like she wanted to be.

"Then we should get rid of it," Chase suggested.

"Obviously we're not getting rid of it." Savage shook her head. "It's too valuable."

Chase looked annoyed, but nobody really wanted to get rid of the thing. Codebreaker schmodebreaker; even the non-idealists among them wanted compensation for their effort.

Ryu said, "It didn't do anything inside here. I think it stalled the pod, but after looking at some diagnostics, I don't think we were ever in any danger. It kind of 'glitched' everything and that made the pod stop like some sort of reset. I've had to shore up some of the barriers between systems to keep us running, but that shouldn't be a problem next time."

Tenor looked knowingly at Locus. *Sure.* Ryu *shored up some systems.* He probably just covered his tracks, like hiding the little spy he surely had to have.

"Nothing vital," Ryu continued. "Nothing dangerous."

Unless you count opening the weapons locker. Unless you count exposing Ryu's treachery. Both of those things happened, by Tenor's reckoning, at the exact time the box hit zero.

But what did that mean, in the context of all that had been said?

Tenor couldn't exactly bring it up to ask.

That was okay, though. It really only mattered that the box had, upon reaching zero, exposed Ryu's treachery to Tenor, thereby giving him the means to stage a coup and deal with the situation. He didn't understand why the log showed Locus's gun unlocking a while after his own, but that was also a stroke of much needed luck.

"So what do we do?" Twilight asked.

"We've got five hours to answer that question and need

about that long to recharge the pod anyway," Ryu said. "So I suggest we get some sleep."

But Tenor couldn't sleep. Nor did he want to. So instead, he waited an hour or so until everyone was either snoring or distracted. Daemon took custody of the box and Ryu went about reviewing logs from the heist, nominally trying to understand what the hell had happened back there.

Ryu's goal was probably more sinister. He was probably collating the valuable info they had, then lighting up his secret antenna array to rat them all out. Soon the black ship — or, hell, maybe NAU Protective Services — would come knocking.

Their new visitors would kill or arrest everyone except Ryu and perhaps Savage, who Tenor was starting to think might be in on the double-cross, then put the black box into the wrong hands.

"So you're saying we need to do this NOW?" Locus asked.

"No time like the present," Tenor said.

He approached Ryu from behind. Locus, who at least had some military brains, positioned himself where he could see all of the others or at least the doors they'd vanished behind. Thanks to weapons locker protocol, the only possible threat would come from blunt objects, not slamguns or slumberguns or plain old bullet guns. Try to use an unlocked weapon — even if the weapons locker was open, which it wasn't — and a host of grizzly security protocols kicked in.

Most guns fired forward. The ones Ryu modified for the heist could also fire backward, if used locked or by the wrong hand. He'd done it because in the original plan, they were supposed to be the only people with conventional, lead-slinging weapons. Ryu's jammer could mute slam weapons same as DZPD's, but if someone dropped their gun and a guard picked it up, that would be bad.

Protections were the answer. And thanks to good fortune, right now Tenor and Locus had the only operational, safe-to-them guns aboard. This should be an easy fight. They could even just shoot Ryu and get on with it.

"Hands up," Tenor said.

Ryu turned, but at first he didn't react.

"Didn't you hear me? Hands up!"

"What's happening?" Ryu asked.

Savage lifted her head from a common-area bunk.

Locus aimed at her, but her eyes didn't settle. That one was trouble. More than the rest of them put together.

"What's going on is I'm taking over."

Ryu laughed.

"I'm serious!" Tenor raised the gun. He'd forgotten to do that before. Stupid mistake, and now he looked like a dickhead.

Ryu saw that this was a threat backed with lead and his mood changed. His hands went up, but only partway.

"Tenor. What are you doing?"

"I told you. I'm taking charge."

"You need to put that gun down."

"You need to eat shit!" Dammit. That was the opposite of clever. Tenor might as well have said that he was rubber and Ryu was glue.

Twilight emerged from a room resisting a half-yawn. She looked at the tableau and said, "What the hell?"

Tenor tossed his chin at Ryu, then spoke to Twilight. "He's the one who ratted us out. He told Xenia we were coming."

"What?" Ryu said. "What the hell?"

"It's true. How else did they know? Where did all that private security come from? Where were the cops? I checked the feed; that little gadget decoded a few bits of DZPD chatter. They didn't even respond to a call at Xenia. Know why? There wasn't even an *alarm* at the labs!"

"So?" Twilight asked.

"Don't you see? He sold us out! Private security! Who else would it be but ..." Dammit. He should have planned this speech. "The mob!"

"What mob?"

"Null!" Yes, that troublesome group of hackers made an excellent punching bag. "Integer7!"

"That wasn't null," said Twilight. "Use your head."

Tenor kept waving his weapon, annoyed that nobody was scared enough. He cocked his gun. That was the attention-getter.

"Listen to me, Tenor." Ryu now had his hands forward: the universal mark of talking to a crazy person. "I didn't do anything like that."

"Then why were they there? Who were those people?" Tenor realized, all at once and with shocking disappointment, that he was scared out of his goddamned mind. "They came at us like they were waiting! Then they let us go!"

"They didn't let us go."

"They let us go! You all saw it!" Tenor pointed to the engines with his free hand, his argument devolving by the second. "He's got an antenna array back there. He's sending our information to someone."

"What?" Chase sounded incensed. Finally, someone willing to believe him. He ran to a panel and started opening system controls, all of which now seemed to be unlocked by the box. "Where?"

Tenor told him, but for some idiot reason Chase found nothing.

He waved his gun at Daemon. "You find it."

But Daemon didn't find anything either.

"I'm telling the truth!" Tenor yelled.

"Put the gun down," Savage said.

"I'll kill him and prove it myself! Even if I have to dig that antenna out with my bare hands!"

Savage was still at a control panel. She looked up as if bitten. "Tenor. Listen to me."

"Fuck that!"

She was undaunted. "Listen to me. Your gun is armed."

"I know it's armed!"

"I mean it's armed *against you.* It's locked." She looked at Locus. "Yours too."

"What?" said Locus.

"Don't listen to her!" Tenor yelled.

"It's true," said Twilight, peering over Savage's shoulder at the weapons display Tenor couldn't see. "I don't know how you got those things out of the locker, but pull the trigger and it's all over."

"Goddamn right it is!"

Something small and annoying was crawling up and down his spine, demanding Tenor's attention. It felt like doubt. Like uncertainty.

But he'd come too far; this way had to be right, no matter what.

"Put it down," Savage said, coming toward him.

"No!"

Chase was moving toward Locus.

Tenor shouted a warning, but the big galoot didn't know what to do.

"Put it down, Tenor," Savage repeated.

"NO!"

She went for Tenor's weapon.

Chase, who'd been watching, went for—

Locus pulled the trigger.

The report, rather than blowing out the muzzle, detonated the weapon's casing. The detonation was directional, bullet and shrapnel both sprayed back like deadly metal rain, turning Locus's face into raw meat on a bone kebab.

Let go. Let go. Put it down.

But his finger was jittering, and his nerves high. He pressed the trigger by what was, strictly speaking, an accident. The result was no less deadly.

But Tenor didn't die instantly like Locus had.

Instead, he had ten seconds of screaming agony.

Just long enough to see the black box blink with a light.

He was the only one who saw it, and the blinking lasted only a second.

The timer was still counting down, now under three and a half hours remaining, but the top line had changed.

It now read, ITERATION 4 OF 11.

Four down, seven to go.

And that was Tenor's final thought.

Chapter Five

SMOKE

SIX MONTHS EARLIER

THE PLACE WASN'T BAD. Good food, white tablecloths, decent but not extravagant wine, and a short, middle-of-the-bell-curve waiter named Brennan who was more flamboyant than Smoke was used to seeing in her line of work.

Brennan had fat little hands, a gem-encrusted pinky ring, and a fuchsia pocket square. He wore a smile that, despite its genuineness, made Smoke want to trip him. Nobody was that happy — especially not waiting tables … and *especially* not waiting tables on terms that Ryu would have explained, because otherwise it'd be cruel.

Or maybe the conditions of today's job *were* what made Brennan so happy in the first place — not because the gig was delightful, but because it ended with a do-over. Few people got genuine do-overs in life. Brennan would soon be the exception.

Ryu had modified Quark-issue nanobots (the kind used by NPS swarmkeepers) to induce a specific kind of memory loss in the group's waiter. If Brennan had followed Ryu's preparatory instructions (no contact the day before; don't leave the house; tell nobody where you are and make no appointments or calls), tomorrow would line up next to yesterday like two puzzle pieces neatly snapping together.

Brennan could live today as freely as he wanted, holding nothing back, because tomorrow, today would no longer exist. He'd never know he'd even lived it, let alone spent it waiting on a table full of revolutionaries. He'd die feeling one day younger than his actual age. Smoke, who loved music, kept thinking of it as life lived with a hidden track.

"More wine?"

Smoke put a hand over the top of her glass, then shook her head at their waiter. She'd had too much already. Tenor, two seats further around the circle, was on his second bottle and not even wobbly. He'd popped an EndLax so he could eat and drink all he wanted, but Smoke thought that was in poor taste.

Ryu wasn't wealthy. Until the job paid off, he was footing the bill for everything himself. It was respectful to eat and drink only what you needed, not act like an entitled asshole devouring every morsel in sight.

Smoke found EndLax repulsive anyway. Something designed for the rich to eat all the fancy food they wanted while the poor starved in the streets. This table should be better than that. Were they not freedom fighters? Wasn't their mission about equality?

Not that Tenor's obliviousness surprised her. The guy was a total dick.

"Come on, Smoke," Tenor said when he saw her looking at him. "When else are you ever going to get a chance to drink Wild East wine? I'm sick of chardonnay.

And cabernet. And chardonnay. And cabernet. This Barolo is out of this world."

"Brunello, actually," Brennan corrected.

"Did anyone fucking ask you?" Tenor snapped. Then to the others: "They're the same thing anyway."

"Brunello de Montalcino," Brennan continued, clearly too chipper. "They're super different!"

Tenor was still staring at the waiter's back even after the door closed.

"Damn," said Asp, adjusting his eyepatch. "I thought we were going to see a Spider situation."

"What spider?" Nero looked like he'd just come from an office. One where they sold gallon-sized jugs of boring. You could set a watch by his neatly parted haircut. His voice was dry and toneless, like he was narrating a 20th-century detective novel.

"*Goodfellas,*" said Asp.

"*Which* fellas?"

"You know. Spider. The waiter. Shot in the foot."

"Who shot who in the what now?" asked Chase.

"'Go get your fuckin' shine box!'" Asp seemed to be quoting something obscure, like always.

"*What?*"

Asp waved a disappointed hand at the table.

"Don't worry about it," Twilight said. "*Let* Tenor make an ass out of himself. If that waiter tells anyone about this, it'll be Tenor he remembers best."

"He won't tell anyone." Ryu was picking asparagus from his plate, eating them by hand. He hadn't looked up, as if he saw the discussion as beneath him.

"You know what I mean," Twilight said.

"I'm not sure I do," Ryu told her, finally looking up. "You either trust me or you don't. Which is it?"

"It was just a joke."

"I'll say it, then," said Savage.

Smoke was surprised. Savage had been the first to hop on board, and now it looked like she was about to raise an objection.

"I don't understand why you're taking the risk. Anyone who has any idea who we are would call NPS just because we're all in the same place at the same time. You want us together, fine. I'm confident in my jammers and I'm sure the rest are too. But this should have been handled by a canvas and AI. Not a human being."

"I already explained—"

"I know. 'The importance of breaking bread.' 'The old ways are lost.' I know you think you can erase his memory—"

"I can. I will. The nanos are already in his brain."

"—but it's just one more loose end, isn't it? If I'm being honest, it's giving me pause."

"About the mission?"

"About your judgment. If we're to trust our lives to you, I think you need to explain why having a human waiter was important enough to risk exposure."

The table waited.

Smoke knew at least part of the answer.

Ryu was normally a ghost. But before he did business with anyone, he liked to look them in the eye, turning the ghost into a real man through a series of very complicated, very paranoid steps. With the Beam controlling so much these days, the only way to know real truths was to rely on the few things The Beam couldn't replicate, like human intuition.

Artificial intelligence came close, but AI intuition had an accent: a specific *kind* of instinct that betrayed a specific kind of non-human logic.

Ryu could tell the difference. He'd brought them

together because that was the first step, and Smoke for one had needed to jump through many hoops before earning her clearance to sit at this table. None of them would leave each other's company until the job was over. You had to bash your way into the inner circle with Ryu, then never leave it. That was the reason for the gathering, and almost certainly the reason for a real waiter — someone whose eyes he could look into.

"He's here because he is not The Beam."

"What's that supposed to mean?" Daemon had wires sticking out of his head. He'd been, Smoke had decided, hot-hacking his brain throughout the meal the same way normal people twiddled their thumbs. His plate had been pushed away and his setting was full of machine parts and wafer chips. Smoke assumed he hadn't even been paying attention.

"As with anything, with The Beam, there is how much the public knows" — Ryu held a hand flat, parallel to the table — "and how much the government and authorities know." He held a second hand above the other. "But in this case, there is also what Quark knows." He moved his lowest hand so it was much higher even than the government hand.

"Conspiracy theory," Rogue said to Twilight, only half-quiet.

Ryu eyed them, then had to stand to move yet another hand higher than Quark. "But what I'm really worried about is all the way up here. *What Noah West knows.*"

Asp laughed.

"You think it's funny."

"Considering West is dead, yes."

"Since before I was born," Chase added.

"You don't have to believe me," Ryu said.

"Good," Tenor whispered to Savage, who wasn't

doubtful enough to join him on any side. She half-rolled her eyes.

"But you *do* have to obey me. You'll do as I say if you want the job."

"And if we don't?" Asp asked Ryu.

He ticked his head toward the door. "Then I erase your memory today, same as Brennan out there. No harm, no foul. The erasure goes back twenty-four hours. That's why we're here so soon after I contacted you. If anyone wants to bail, the rest of us can rest assured that you won't remember being contacted this morning."

Smoke considered pushing back, but it was always Ryu's way or the highway. Based on what she'd heard so far, she wanted in. This job would be a feather in her cap, a crapload of universal credits in her proxied bank account, and might even do a whole lot of good for the world.

So right now that meant not rocking the boat.

Ryu continued. "Believe me or don't, but I'm quite sure The Church of West is right about one thing. Noah's imprint is still out there. And if it is, it's one hell of a lot smarter by now than the company he founded or the network he invented. I don't know what he knows. There's no way I even could. But I *do* know that if we don't take precautions against 'what we don't know we don't know' about West or the Beam or anything else, this could end before it even gets started."

"Bullshit," said Locus, at Smoke's side, holding her hand under the table.

"Null knows there was an upload right before Noah West died. Integer7 says he's seen proof."

"I've seen Bigfoot," said Asp. "Big fuckin' deal. Integer7 could be an NPS spook for all we know."

Ryu shook his head. Smoke, for one, thought Ryu

might even *be* Integer7. If not, the two hackers and innovators were equals, at least.

"Even if there was a West imprint once upon a time, it's totally fragmented," Twilight said. "A trillion bits of data, scattered across the entire network."

"It's like I said," Ryu kept going, "you can believe me or not, but *do as I say* if you want to stay. You all know my reputation. I don't think you'd be here if you didn't. Creating within the Quark corporate sandbox has shown me a lot of things that aren't widely known, which is why *I'm* here. Technology is supposed to be an equalizer, but Quark and Xenia are keeping the best stuff for themselves and their friends. It's our job to change that — to crack Xenia's servers and make their entire inventory open-source."

Ryu took a beat to make sure everyone was listening, then he continued.

"Think about it. Quark's network has evolved exponentially, and yet we've only seen linear add-on growth for the past decade or so. That right there should prove that they're not letting the public see the most cutting-edge peripherals. I've only had glimpses myself, tossing a few crawlers into lesser sectors on the Quark side of the firewall, but the tech gap is about to become dangerous. The powerful have always looked for ways to get more power. Soon, there won't be any way of stopping it."

"What's dangerous?" Rogue asked.

"I've seen the immersion rigs Xenia makes for Beau Monde clients. They plug right into the brain."

"Like in *The Matrix*," said Asp.

"It's not differentiable from real life," Ryu kept going, ignoring Asp like everyone else. "They have nanobots called Series Six that can do all sorts of things most people still think of as science fiction. They can down-tune natural senses and proprioception and balance, for one, so that when you're in a top-tier immersion, you can't feel the real world at all. The Beau Monde eye mods can see through walls — not because they're X-ray eyes, but because they pull data from Beam-connected sources on the wall's other side and show it to the user directly. Everything seen and heard and felt by everyone on the streets and all patrols and all loose hover nanos ... all that stuff combines to form a copy of the physical world in virtual space. With Xenia add-ons and Quark nanobots, immersive VR could be used to enter any space, even if it's locked and prohibited. Do you see the problem?"

"Omnipresent surveillance?"

"For one," said Ryu.

"That's not so dangerous." Tenor shook his head.

"Skills uploads. Mind transfers."

"More sci-fi," Locus said.

"No. It's real. This is all coming off of Project Mindbender a while back. I assume you all remember that?"

Smoke's smile vanished.

So did everyone else's.

Now Ryu really had their attention. "They talk about the 'dislocation paradigm' all the time inside the firewall. That's Mindbender talk. Apparently, they're close to solving it. They'll have effective immortality once they do. Someone whose mind is backed up multiple servers and has Xenia duplicate bodies lined up for download can no longer die. If you think the social gap is large now, just wait."

Smoke looked toward the door. She already knew the reasons to do the job in the first place. Equality for all plus a big fat payday for every one of the eleven people around the table.

Thinking too long about the stakes made her heavier

than she wanted to feel right now, and Smoke wasn't a weak person. Time to dial this back, remember where this tangent had begun in the first place.

The waiter. Ryu's judgment. The question of how blindly they should follow their leader.

Twilight spoke next. "You're saying that if we end our Beam block-out …"

"We'll be wide open," Ryu finished, nodding. He cocked his thumb. "I can erase Brennan. I can't erase what I don't know is there. The building is an enhanced Faraday cage. No signals in or out. If we play dead, keeping off The Beam, we'll stay in the black hole I've made for us. It's a dead spot in the Internet of Things. I got us a human waiter for the same reason I use pen and paper. Digital gives us away. Paper and squishy organics?" He nodded. "Those things are safe. Might as well tell me now, and save us all some time. Any of you guys want out? Anyone here lost interest?"

Nobody spoke.

So Ryu began. He explained the reason he'd decided to gather a crew and take on the mission. The socially conscious worry that if the rich and powerful kept getting the best tech while the middle class and poor got less, only the rich would matter. And soon.

Right now, Ryu was waging a good fight against the Xenias and Quarks of the world, acting as a counterbalance because whatever Xenia made, Ryu improved. There was more and more lately, though, that Ryu couldn't even see behind Xenia's firewall. He couldn't keep up — and the more he failed to keep pace with Xenia, the faster and faster the company could innovate.

Without the world's Ryus to act as checks and balances, the NAU would become a god-state. The upper class wouldn't even need to be present to oppress them all.

Revolution after that wouldn't be just difficult. It wouldn't even be impossible. Instead, it would be something worse: *irrelevant.*

The word itself would cease to make sense.

Ryu explained the plan. They'd enter Xenia Labs, each of their party with a specific job to do. Rogue already had access to a Stark suit — part of the supposed-to-be-secret-but-not-to-Ryu program that Quark called Centurion. The suit was essential. It was impervious to just about any weapon other than flung lead, which had gone extinct in the NAU fifteen years earlier thanks to a governmental crackdown on "non mutable" weaponry and quadrillions of nanobot inspectors conducting density analysis.

Rogue, wearing the suit, would take point and act as a shield. Based on Xenia intel that Ryu had been buying and hacking his way into for a couple of years now, they'd barely need anyone else — at least not for the physical part of the job.

The others would support the Stark suit's thrust.

Chase was the charmer, distracting anyone who could be distracted.

Asp didn't give a shit about anything; he was the one who'd go in guns blazing.

Smoke and Twilight were weapons experts; they'd be in charge not just of arming the group with the Wild East lead-flingers Ryu had amassed and risked his life to hide, but of modifying shield generators on the fly as Xenia's guards (and, probably, DZPD) moved their slamguns into rotating frequencies.

Nero was an investigator; Daemon was tech fabrication and wouldn't go into the field; Locus was on-site intel thanks to his enhanced specs (plus muscle. The man was a beast). Savage was demolition as needed, and a general badass otherwise.

Ryu would obviously call the shots. And Tenor? Smoke figured he was there because every group needed a wild-card. If things went bad, his trigger-happy, quick-to-anger impulsiveness might save their asses. If they were chased, Smoke also took comfort in knowing she could shoot him in the leg to slow the cops down. Let them take Tenor's lagging ass instead of everyone else.

"And once we're inside …" Smoke started.

"We drop the firewall," Twilight finished.

Ryu shook his head. "We make our physical attack first. Phase two is the technological attack. That part happens off-site the next day."

"Wait," Smoke said. "Why would we break in if we aren't planning to hack from inside the firewall?"

"I can get at most of Xenia's protections without leaving my shop," Ryu explained. "I've seen enough to know I'm never going to get through them with my current knowledge and tools. The encryption itself has changed. It's not a matter of effort; it's a matter of total and complete inability."

"If you can't break the codes, why are we doing this?" Savage asked.

"Because we're there for something that *can* break them. I need the codemaker pool."

Ryu explained about the files in the protected, isolated clean room. There was no hard connection to The Beam, so a person could only get at that room by physically entering the space. They weren't at Xenia to break the database open for the world to see. They were there to get the master key, which they'd use once back home.

As far as jobs went, Ryu's plan sounded like cake to Smoke. Without the need to linger and infiltrate, they'd be in and out in ten minutes with their Stark suit, Ryu-made slamgun shields, and unexpected ammunition — the simplest payday any of them would ever have.

And he promised a *massive* payday. Based on what Ryu could see without full access, Xenia had over eleven thousand high-end designs set aside for the Beau Monde. They could stash ten or twenty for themselves before opening the floodgates, then sell them to the Wild East.

The NAU wouldn't miss those few designs and the Wild East was too impoverished and fragmentary to pose any threat. Only governments had money outside the NAU, and they'd pay most of it to Ryu for fancy inventions that couldn't hurt anyone. A nice side effect would be bankrupting governments that might otherwise buy bluntly destructive weapons, like nano-cluster-mapped nuclear warheads. Win-win for everyone.

No one left. Ryu announced that although he was paying for dinner, funds for the alcohol had been donated by a Ryu-friendly crowdfunding campaign on the null hyperforum. Smoke assumed he'd waited to reveal this until after everyone had agreed, so nobody was consenting drunk.

Inebriation reigned after that. Even Ryu loosened up.

Smoke alone didn't partake. She was a lightweight and didn't enjoy feeling out of control. So as the others got drunker, she held onto her dawning sobriety. This was intentional, especially after a while.

Some people, like Asp, were cavalier. Smoke never had been. She'd been meek once, in her twenties, before giving birth to her son. She'd been part of a revolutionary group then, because her husband was a smuggler, Smoke wanting nothing to do with guns and particle weapons and moon-dust junkies and violence.

She planned on moving her son to a calm suburban life once her man died, which he absolutely would given the group's activities, and which he did just after John turned ten. The only flaw in her plan was that when a rival band took her husband's life, they took her son as well.

Smoke hadn't seen him since, and now she was nearly sixty years old.

That day had stolen the last of her meekness and made her hard like leather. She didn't trust easily and rarely lowered her guard. Instead, Smoke remained aware of her surroundings. Forever vigilant, always learning the exits and keeping the clearest head in any room, because that was how you held your perimeter.

In drink, she saw their true personalities.

Tenor and Chase were both proud. They talked big because they felt small. It meant they couldn't be counted on. Fear could get them running, especially if they believed that no one would see. They were hotheads, easily provoked and hard to reason with. She planned to keep an eye on them both.

Nero was solid. He kept his head down and did his job. There was no flash to the man, which Smoke took for a good thing. His only failing was his need for respect. Nero wanted his contributions to be acknowledged. She'd keep his allegiance in the simplest way possible: *by telling him he was great.*

Locus was sweet and she liked him a lot, but she'd need to watch his back while watching her own. He was big and strong and good-hearted, believing in the mission more than the money. But his trust in the others revealed his naiveté — something that exposed itself even more as he drank. Truth was, Locus wasn't as smart as the others. She'd need to keep close, and ensure that no shiny pennies lured his spectacled eyes.

Rogue and Daemon partnered off as the evening wore on. She caught snippets of their conversation as she milled, pretending to be as inebriated as everyone else while drinking juice Brennan kept bringing her — all with a delightful *shush* about him, as if his happy self was delighted to be in on her deception.

Rogue and Daemon were both tech-mired … a term the eggheads used to describe a phase before full-on tech addiction. There were many people who couldn't get through an hour without The Beam — without its ever-present, always-omniscient sensors and surfaces to detect their wants and fill them instantly. Both men claimed, in a drunken huddle, that they'd get through Ryu's required Beam blackout the same way Ryu himself would. By tinkering with disconnected peripherals, relying on a cloned Beam sector that behaved much the same but without nearly as much reach. It would be enough, they seemed to think.

Smoke, who knew better than most how bad Beam withdrawal could be, made a mental note to keep her eye on them.

Asp was a loner. She'd known that, but Drunk Asp turned out to be pretty much the same as Sober Asp, meaning little of his personality was an act. That was good in some ways (what you saw from Asp was what you got), but loners didn't always work well in groups. He hadn't seemed to trust Smoke when he met her, or now. It'd only been a few hours, so maybe that was normal.

Savage was perhaps the most solid of the recruits, and Smoke spent the most time with her over the course of their inaugural evening. Savage was also a mother, though her kids were in their late teens and part of the Harajuku cell she herself had come from. Neither woman liked to open up fully, but Savage's … well … *savagery* made Smoke feel like her tough-girl persona was only an act.

Savage looked and sounded like a person who could

eat iron and shit rivets. She was fully sold on the plan from an idealist standpoint — enough that it scared Smoke a little. Savage didn't even want her full share of the money. She planned to collect it, then give almost all of it away to the information-freedom cause. What worried Smoke about Savage was that the mission clearly mattered more to her than the people. She wanted tech equality even more than Ryu, and if she had to kill them all to ensure the success of her mission, Smoke felt she'd do it without blinking.

Still, Smoke liked her better than Twilight. She was an idealist, too, but Twilight talked like a victim. The group's male dominance didn't threaten Smoke or Savage, but it seemed to bother Twilight a lot. She kept announcing oppression where Smoke saw none. It made her edgy and paranoid. Twilight could slip if she felt insulted, and slips on a job like this could cost lives.

Somehow Smoke forgot about Ryu until the very end, because their leader was quiet. Ryu, it seemed, was the only other member of the party not drinking. He made Smoke reach for her heart when she spotted him, his hard brown eyes watching her observing the others.

That's when she realized this drunken game wasn't only hers. Ryu hadn't *allowed* his group to drink; he'd *intended* for it to. This was a test for the others in his eyes, same as it was a test for the others in hers.

Smoke settled next to him. Fifteen minutes later, he spoke to her with respect in his voice. While the others were busy exposing their truest selves, Smoke had been gathering data, same as him.

That's how wars were won: with information, not strong arms.

"You wanted to watch them," Smoke said.

Ryu shook his head. "I need to know what will undo them."

Chapter Six

TWILIGHT

Twilight touched the box.

She did it exactly like they'd showed her, and the display came right up.

"Savage," she said, looking at it.

Savage was reading on one of Ryu's modified tablets. The tablets here were dead things, more useful as blunt weapons with their connectivity off, but they did have content downloaded to them. Twilight could have used one as well, but she hadn't felt much like listening to music or watching movies. She certainly hadn't felt like reading. How Savage could kick back with a book when there were still bits of Tenor and Locus all over the floor, she had no idea.

Twilight was more than preoccupied, playing it all back. She hated seeing the gore, which had gone from bright red to something near black as it dried. Since considered cleaning it up since she couldn't relax. She'd stopped when she spotted Chase watching her, about to make a comment. He lived a century in the past, back when people still talked about "women's work."

Maybe it was his Wild East upbringing. Twilight didn't know, but she'd be damned if she'd let him see her cleaning. Maybe she should climb onto the console and jiggle her tits for him instead. Asshole.

Right now, the box was occupying her plenty.

Savage had her big black boots kicked onto the console's edge. She looked like she didn't want to get up, then did. She seemed taller when she reached Twilight's side, though much shorter.

"What?"

"Look." Twilight again slid her hands down the box's sides. The display, which had gone dark, reappeared.

Savage looked. "So?"

"You don't think that's strange?"

"No. An hour ago, there was an hour more left. I'm familiar with the way time passes."

Twenty minutes until zero. Ryu had theories as to why the box was counting down, but they all sounded like blue-sky guesses to Twilight — the way people hypothesized where souls went after dying.

"That's not what I'm talking about." She pointed at the other line on the display. "I mean this."

"'Iteration 4 of 11,'" Savage read. "So?"

"It read '2 of 11' before."

Savage already looked bored. "What are you talking about?"

"Well, an 'iteration' is like an attempt at something, right? Or a cycle. You do something once, it's the first iteration. You do it again, that's the second iteration."

"Again, *so?*"

"When did it go through two more iterations? It hasn't gone to zero again. I figure that's a cycle."

"Who cares?"

"You don't think it makes sense that hitting zero would mark a new iteration?"

"I don't know. It's not my box."

Twilight saw the problem.

The box could be grabbing them by the necks and smashing them into things and Savage still wouldn't care. She wasn't intellectually curious. She only cared about two things: the mission and survival. Survival was either automatic or moot (no need to sweat anything if you failed that one), so that meant all she *truly* carried about was redistributing technology and, as a result, wealth.

Her parents had died outside a low-end Enterprise hospital, too broke to go inside and too broke in the first place to afford the nanobot treatments that even the middle class took like vitamins.

Savage went to Xenia to find a way to break the codes keeping all those tech goodies in wealthy hands and level the playing field for folks like her parents, but instead they'd found something much more powerful. That right there was all that mattered to Savage.

Ryu didn't even understand what the box did, other than absolutely everything. Right now it seemed the thing could break any code without so much as touching the hardware. If that was true, there'd soon be no more secrets in District Zero. If that was true, anything else the box did — to Savage, at least — was irrelevant.

But it bothered Twilight. She couldn't precisely say why, other than the fact that she was truly, deeply frightened but couldn't show it because Chase was always right there looking at her, waiting for her to show weakness.

She was bottled up and the only other woman had an assassin's emotions. If she said any of this to any of the men, they'd probably laugh at her.

Look at little Twilight — afraid it'll go boom!

Nobody else seemed bothered. Last time the box went to zero, it called a goddamn dreadnought to hover over their heads.

What kind of a ship was that, anyway? She imagined it full of the same black-suited guards they'd met inside Xenia — the ones who weren't supposed to be there, who fired real bullets, who clearly knew Ryu's group was coming, and from whom they'd somehow escaped under suspicious circumstances.

The connection between the box and the black ship didn't seem by-the-way in the least to Twilight. It felt like a leash.

Maybe they *hadn't* actually escaped those strange guards.

Maybe they just thought they had, and it was only a matter of time before their captors reeled in the tether.

Twilight suddenly wanted very badly to get rid of the box. There was so much wrong about it. At best the device was giving away their location. At worst, it might yet do what strange boxes did when their timers hit zero in the movies.

Maybe she could dump it without anyone seeing, and screw the consequences.

But what would happen then? The black-jacket guards had surrounded the box at Xenia and were still surrounding it now. If she jettisoned the thing now, they'd take it right back. Then goodbye mission, hello technological autocracy.

Ryu was right; the digital gap was growing at an exponential rate. This might be their only chance to stop it. If Twilight chickened out of this game of Hot Potato, there might be no NAU left.

She'd be poor. They all would be. There were a whole

lot of credits at the end of this particular rainbow, but not if she tossed their cargo and ran.

"There are eleven of us," Twilight said quietly. "Or *were*. Now there are six."

"Are you kidding?" Savage asked.

No. She wasn't kidding. Four down, seven to go; that's what the display told her.

The only glitch was Nero, who hadn't weighed in on either side.

But that was ridiculous, right?

"They deserved it, you know," Savage said.

Twilight had been looking down. Her eyes rose, meeting Savage's.

She'd never noticed; Savage had soft blue-green eyes, not the hard black pellets she'd been assuming from a distance. Pretty eyes. It made Savage feel like a real person for the first time. Before — to Twilight — she'd seemed more like a machine, without heart or feeling.

"What?"

"Tenor and Locus. They deserved what they got."

"How can you say that?"

"Because it's true. Doesn't matter that we sat around for months with them. Doesn't matter if Locus ever brought you a cup of coffee or said hi in the morning. Doesn't matter if Tenor had a secret soft side. What matters is they both died waving guns in our faces. They made their choices, and they got what sons of bitches get."

"I wasn't wondering about—"

"Sure you were. You've been sitting in that chair for over two hours now, staring at the blood. You feel guilty about everything, but this one isn't anyone's fault but theirs."

Twilight supposed that was true. Still, she didn't particularly care to confirm Savage's theory so she settled for not denying it instead.

"So the box is counting. That's what intelligent code-makers do. In …" Savage looked. "Sixteen minutes and four seconds, it's going to hit zero. Maybe it'll call that ship again, and maybe it'll come back. That's why Ryu's stopped charging and is spooling up to jump. We just need to stay ahead of it like last time, then I suppose we'll get another six hours to figure things out. *If* that's even what's happening. But I see you looking at that readout and at the puddle of assholes who tried to take over and kill us. It's like you think they're connected. They're not. We didn't even have eleven people when we took it, remember? Smoke and Rogue were already dead. Maybe Nero, too."

"But …"

"I'm not interested. I suggest you stop being interested, too. This is a big win. You get that, right? I talked to Ryu. He's been combing through the pod's system logs, trying to understand what happened six hours ago when we just went dead. He says the pod didn't just shut down. It didn't just 'unlock.' It didn't 'decode itself' and that's all there is to it. He and Daemon keep finding places where the code has actually been *rewritten*. Decoding the pod's systems wouldn't really do much other than leave us adrift, but new code that bypasses control and directly connects the engines to the sensors? That would let any kid with a tablet control the pod and make it go wherever she wanted, and there'd be nothing we can do to stop it."

"And that *shouldn't* interest me?" Twilight asked.

"He wrote a patch. He might have to write a new one fifteen minutes from now, if the thing does it again. We'll be fine. But imagine that happening at Enterprise HQ. Imagine it happening at Xenia's secure facility — the one Ryu didn't even want to try and hit because we'd have no chance of bringing it down. Imagine it happening at *Quark*. Or what about the Quark PD wing of the DZPD? What if it 'decodes' the Beam Clerics who work there? Maybe then kids can control *them*."

"Does Ryu actually think that's possible?"

"Clerics are just bodies animated by sentient nanobots. I don't see why it couldn't break their codes, too."

"Jesus."

"Right." Savage slapped her on the shoulder. "So smile, Twilight. We won big today. *And* we found out who not to trust before they could do any real damage." She looked at the dried blood, and Twilight couldn't help thinking that Locus had grabbed a gun but he didn't strike her as a saboteur. Locus was malleable, and easily swayed. Losing Smoke had unseated him, wrecked his stability. "I don't like losing people any more than anyone else, but they brought it on themselves. So maybe stop worrying. You're seeing stuff that isn't there."

Twilight's hands were still on the box. Without meaning to, she re-woke its display.

"And hey," Savage said when she saw it, "look on the bright side. If I'm wrong, it'll all be over in thirteen minutes."

Savage left her, seeming to think her job of reassuring Twilight was over.

But she didn't feel reassured. Master key or not, Twilight didn't like this box. Maybe it was the secret-buster that the others wanted, but to her the thing had terrible energy. To her, it wasn't inert rock and it wasn't full of quantum circuitry.

No, there was something alive inside. Something she didn't like. Something that she'd swear was watching her. Watching all of them. Counting them off. Playing games until checkmate, when the beast in its guts could finally break out of its chrysalis.

She looked at the readout. Just over twelve minutes left.

She could still do something. Nobody was looking; she could walk the box right out the pod's door, then throw it into a field.

Or, better: she could throw it into the capacitor array Ryu had set up to quick-charge the pod's batteries.

They'd all want to kill her, but that would be okay. At least it'd be gone. At least the creeping feeling on the back of her neck would no longer have a source, and the devil you knew was pretty much always better than the devil you didn't.

She picked it up. She was going to do this.

Everyone else was willing to roll with the weird shit surrounding this box, but not Twilight. Savage said this might be their last chance to bring down the Beau Monde and whatever secret upper classes might exist above even them? Well, before they got that far, she had another last chance to consider.

If Twilight didn't get rid of the box now, the world would have it forever.

It's a Trojan horse, and they want to bring it right on inside.

Not if she had anything to say about it.

The box was smooth-sided and her hands were sweating profusely. As Twilight rose, the thing slid in her hands.

She caught the box before dropping it, but the display came alight when she did:

ITERATION 4 OF 11

00:11:33

Then, below that, a new line.

VARIABLE INCOMING.

"Savage?" she said again.

But there was a knock on the door before she could answer.

Chapter Seven

NERO

Nero kept wanting to say he was too old for this shit.

It seemed appropriate. He'd been a cop in a former life, and he'd even worked right under current chief Dominic Long, though back then Dominic had only been a sergeant. Cops were always saying they were too old for various kinds of shit, and neither Dominic nor Nero, both of whom looked their ages unlike most people today, were exceptions.

It wasn't the only thing they'd had in common, either.

From the first time Nero saw Dominic, he knew the other man had a secret. Dominic was too honest for a cop, but in a very specific way — one that seemed steeped in justified borderline morality.

Nero was pretty sure Captain Long was somehow involved in Lunis smuggling, for instance, but if so he made no money from the endeavor. More importantly, Nero had noticed the name Long had given his handheld and, he suspected, the terminal canvas in his office at the station. *Chrissy*.

Something had scratched at Nero's instincts about that name and the oddly cordial way Long interacted with his computer's personality, so Nero snooped. Turned out Long once had a sister, born before state eugenics with some sort of a developmental condition that mandated her, eventually, to execution by Respero.

But Chrissy Long disappeared before that could happen. It was a tempting string to pull, because although people could still vanish in the first part of the century, they were much harder to erase in 2097. Nero let it go, because he didn't care for the Respero system, especially when it came to people who couldn't help what they were. It was one of the reasons he'd left the force. One of the reasons he'd assumed a new profession.

The cops would say he was a criminal now, but he'd quit because he didn't agree with cop labels to begin with. They called him a fugitive. Nero, like Savage, preferred to see himself as a freedom fighter.

Thinking of Dominic Long and his departed sister as he hobbled across open ground to the backup rendezvous point, Nero wished he'd taken more with him when he'd left the force. There were files he could have copied. He knew how. Respero in particular had grabbed his attention since, and it was Respero that motivated his part in Ryu's crazy code-stealing adventure.

There were inconsistencies in those Respero records he could still access. It was starting to look like a dumping ground, a deep lake where mob guys dropped bodies. It even looked somehow connected to that ghost in the machine all the nutball anthroposophist, Church-of-West weirdoes wouldn't shut up about: *SerenityBlue.*

And to think, Nero had access to so much Respero data back when he'd worn a badge, and now that he was a rebel against it, he had so little.

Well. Maybe that would change, if Ryu had gotten the codes they'd broken into Xenia for. Maybe he hadn't been shot, three times, for nothing.

The wounds were stable for now. He'd taken one in the leg, one in the shoulder, and one in the neck that had scared the bejesus out of him when he'd first looked in the mirror. A person didn't expect to catch a bullet in the neck.

But Nero was lucky; the shot had punched through a wing of mostly skin, some muscle, and hadn't even left him unable to move his head. With no organ wounds, he'd staunched the bleeding at the first recharge station he'd found that had an exterior bathroom, using a cauterizing stick. After that came the Neuralin injection, which dispatched his shock and anemia with a devastating punch. He'd feel it in the morning, but hopefully by then he could get to an autodoc. A *discrete* autodoc.

Fortunately, Ryu could almost for-sure hook that up.

Physically, Nero was more or less okay. He'd live. He was limping like a man on uneven stilts, but he'd see another day. Emotionally, how Nero felt was a different story. He was forty and looked it, whereas most people in his income bracket looked twenty at forty, and forty when they were kissing a hundred. More importantly, he *felt* forty. He should be spryer than this. He should be able to get shot thrice and skip off laughing, a young buck like himself.

But no. He'd opted out of all nano treatments, also like Dominic Long, obeying some instinct about the easy way being the way wherein Noah West's legacy held you by the nuts for the rest of your life.

Now he had this natural mid-life body, and each step made him moan like an old man rising from his rocker. Women his age didn't want him because he looked too old, and women old enough to be his grandmother hit on him all the time, saying how handsome he was. Sometimes Nero thought, *This is how Benjamin Button must have felt.* But it was never as funny as it should have been.

Definitely too old for this shit.

Nero looked back. He'd stowed his stolen screetbike in a cluster of hedges, reasoning that there might be no room in the barn and he'd have to drive it back to hide it anyway. Now he wished he'd just driven. He'd had adrenaline on his side when he'd bled his way out of Xenia's emergency exit. Now, the adrenaline was gone and despite the Neuralin, he could feel pain and definitely fear. Cop fear (an analytical kind that was a little like a toaster analyzing a romantic movie), but there.

He'd seen that big black hovership a while back, and thought it was chasing him. Paranoid, perhaps, but then again Nero felt sure the guards who'd ambushed them had let him get away. He'd found the police screetbike right outside the door, unlocked and ready to fly, in a spot with no police around. It felt like when Alice came across food and drink in wonderland, and the dumbass gobbled it up.

Still, even knowing how dumb and convenient the whole thing was, Nero took the bike. He'd keep an eye out to be sure he wasn't followed. He'd been a cop; he knew what he was doing.

Only after losing the black ship had he gone to the rendezvous, but still he was reckless. Someone had left that bike for him; someone had wanted him to take it. Ryu, somehow anticipating the need for a backdoor exit, an unknown ally, or (and this was clearly the answer) an enemy who wanted to see where he went.

This was the last place he should be.

But there were extenuating circumstances. Nero needed to tell the others what he'd learned more than he needed to protect them from discovery. At least that's how he was rationalizing this.

They'd caught him. Back at Xenia, they'd caught him for a while. He was shot; he went down; it was the wound in his neck that first time and all the blood made him able to play dead.

The guards approached. They weren't Xenia-native; these boys and girls had come from somewhere else. At first, Nero thought they were Beamers. Except that Beamers wore visored helmets, because they preferred the simulated reality of The Beam to the actual world.

Beamers believed that Beam-delivered reality was truer than the real thing.

The folks who came for Nero, by contrast, were wearing riot gear when he saw them close up. They had no identifiers at all — no badges, no insignia, no nothing — and he'd seen firsthand that their guns were enough to earn automatic Respero for the lot of them. Nero would have said they were mercenaries, maybe smuggled through the NAU border from somewhere in the Wild East. But he changed his mind when the first of them spoke.

They didn't have accents.

They did, however, have flies in their eyes.

Not literally, of course. Nero, on a rare girlfriend's urging, had read her favorite novel — a mid-twentieth-century war parody called *Catch-22*. A character in the book kept saying that one of his platoon-mates had flies in his eyes. It didn't make much sense in the book, but Nero, on reading it, decided that was the perfect way to describe Beam Clerics.

It was, in fact, the way Beam Clerics identified themselves — something they did not as confession, but in order to exert authority.

The NAU was really One Nation Under the Beam. The government and armed forces could pretend they had top billing, but it was the network that controlled the land. The Beam touched everything everywhere except the technophobe Organa villages.

People — especially people who lived in a nexus like District Zero — lived within the network nearly as much as Beamers. They saw the real world with their real eyes, but every surface was painted with Beam screens. Most wore ocular displays and cochlear implants, meaning The Beam ultimately controlled what they knew, heard, believed, and thought.

The Beam opened doors or kept them locked. It told autocabs where to drive, and what to avoid. It touched every mobile, every grafted-on peripheral, every heads-up display, every appliance and information portal in every home above the line. Below the line, even the destitute and homeless had mobiles and tablets — or, failing that, public Beam surfaces. Medical nanobots — in the water and recirculated air supplies and hence present in everyone who wasn't Organa, including abstainers like Nero — talked to each other and to The Beam.

The Beam was above everything. Maybe not in concept, but definitely in practice. That made Beam Clerics the world's trump cards, able to cut through red tape and get answers — to anything — as soon as they identified themselves.

That identification could be done with a flashlight. Just look into a Cleric's eyes and you'd see a few of the millions of nanobots propping up their meat-sack bodies, reflecting light even at microscopic size, like flies in the eyes.

The black-clad guards were Clerics. That explained everything. Somehow something had leaked, and an autonomous agent somewhere on The Beam had decided to interfere with Ryu's plan.

What it didn't explain was why, and why in this way.

Experts all seemed to agree that The Beam, while it could think for itself, was more or less neutral in its allegiance. Some theorized that the AI there had been loyal to Noah West prior to his death, and conspiracy nuts said it was secretly allegiant to one or both of two different people, not Noah, but lunatics like that blathered about all sorts of things.

Either way, The Beam, if it found them out, should have alerted Xenia to block them at the front door rather than letting them inside. It should have called NPS or DZPD on them, not Clerics. And what should Nero make of the Cleric firing physical ammunition? Anyone got a whiff of that, and the scandal would crack society's walnut better than any code Ryu could steal.

Nero found it out when he tried to play possum, then jump the first guard to approach his "dead" body. The few nanobots circulating in Nero's system told the nanos inside the Clerics that he was alive and well, then clustered in his arm to retard the speed of his triceps muscles.

His strike was far too slow and the Cleric guard was prepared. Nero got a chop to his throat for the trouble, and two minutes later he'd had his back to a wall and was sure he was about to be executed firing-squad style.

But he had to fight for his breath when they started asking him questions instead.

Though it was more like a psychic reading than any sort of interrogation.

"You are Blaine Gregorovitch, former District Zero Police Department, born one fourteen fifty-seven," said the first of them. He (it) had the form of a brown-haired man with a dimpled chin. Nero kept wanting to reach out and put his finger into it.

"I go by 'Nero' now, thanks."

Another of the Clerics spoke next, ignoring him. "Citation for valor oh four two one two zero eight eight."

A woman with hair far too nice to have just engaged in a shooting match. They'd worn helmets at first, like Beamers, and Nero knew this one only because she'd taken a huge blot of Smoke's blood on her feet when she'd shot her, then finished her off by plunging four sharpened glove-fingers through her gasping throat.

Nero wanted to hurt her for killing Smoke, but he wanted to ask how she could remain so dedicated to beauty while ending lives even more. He knew the answer; her follicles were obviously crawling with maintenance nanobots.

"Reprimand by Internal Affairs oh four one nine two zero eight eight."

"That was a misunderstanding. IA sent me home with a recommendation for valor when they learned the pieces of shit I beat to death were just a couple of fucking skinbags."

The male Cleric shoved his fist into Nero's crotch and filled it with thousands of volts. Nero was pretty sure he'd seen the last of his testicles, though he'd since verified that they were very much still there.

"You have been apprehended as an enemy of the state. Tell us where the others have gone."

"Touchy, aren't you, for a couple of fucking skinbags?"

More volts to the jimmies. Oh well — he never wanted kids anyway.

"Give the location of your rendezvous."

"Your mom's house."

The man looked to the woman. "That is not correct."

Noah Fucking West. Artificial intelligence indeed.

"Tell us."

"I already told you — your mom is supposed to be there to welcome them in. With her butt cheeks spread."

"You are not telling the truth."

"I mean, she had two extra assholes installed for the occasion, but there's a lot of us, so we're going to have to take turn—"

This time Nero was ready for the shock. He'd pulled his pants askew a bit, dragging his belt buckle low enough for the Cleric to hit it when he tried again. There was a snap, crackle, and a pop, then Nero was up and bending the Cleric's arm back to press his electric fingers into his own chest.

Then he drew the Cleric's gun, aiming it at the female. "Don't move."

The woman said nothing.

"Don't follow me."

Nero ran. Nobody chased him. The screetbike was out back and he was in the clear minutes later, soaring above the traffic line and taking cover in fortuitous low-hanging clouds. It was easy to hit someone up here because traffic-skirters flew in the clouds to reach their destinations faster, but Nero took his chances.

He used the multipurpose tool in his pocket to claw off the bike's guidance module, then replaced it with the coded mobile Ryu had given each of them for emergencies. He'd followed blips to the route, then the route toward the rendezvous.

All at once, near the start of his journey, he'd seen the black ship settled smack-dab along the rendezvous route. He watched more black-clad people — Clerics, probably — emerge. He'd waited and hid, then slowly made his way along.

He'd reached his destination through the world's most circuitous route hours later. Now here he was, minutes from the cutoff time, hobbling into the return of his pain. A balls way to end his trip, but at least he was still alive.

He knocked on the pod's skin, locating it through the cloak with effort.

The door opened with a gun in his face.

"Easy," he said.

Chase lowered the weapon, which Nero was amused to see wasn't even loaded. Or more accurately, the gun was empty. What exactly had they been doing here, if they hadn't so much as reloaded?

"You're alive."

"Astute," Nero decided. "Is your mommy home, little boy?"

Chase stepped aside, but with a sour expression. The two of them had never gotten along for a very simple reason. Nero acted like a professional, whereas Chase acted like a Euro pig with more dicks than sense.

Nero didn't like Chase because he was a disrespectful hothead who didn't seem to think Nero's extensive police experience made him an asset to the mission. Chase didn't like Nero because Chase was a giant bag of shit.

He walked into a who's who. Twilight, holding some sort of odd black box, Savage looking like she'd just finished devouring a cheetah, Daemon with goggles on and a confused expression that somehow affected only his mouth, Asp with a bloody split on one leg, and Ryu hunched over a console, looking hassled if not bagged.

"Where are the others?" Nero asked.

"Rogue and Smoke didn't make it," said Asp. "I got it in the leg."

"I know about Rogue and Smoke."

"And that's Tenor and Locus," said Chase, pointing at

a dark red mess on the floor. They'd all been walking through it. Nero saw tracks everywhere.

"What happened?"

"A disagreement," said Asp. "How the fuck you get back here?'

"I stole a screetbike."

"Really?" Asp clearly didn't believe him. "Where'd you find a screetbike?"

They were all looking at him funny. Like he'd done something wrong.

"It was outside."

"And you found us," Savage said. "No problem."

"Of course I found you. I had the same instructions as everyone else."

Still they all stared.

"What exactly is going on here?" Nero asked.

"How did you start the bike, Nero?" Daemon didn't talk much, so this was a special occasion.

"It was already unlocked."

"And they didn't freeze the area?"

"It's a **DZPD** screetbike. They can't be frozen." He waited a beat. "Noah Fucking West — do you want to see it?"

"No. Just take your seat." Ryu was still fussing with the console. Nero wanted to go closer, to see what he was up to. It looked a bit frantic, like he was afraid of being chased.

"I'd like to see it," said Asp.

Ryu shook his head. "There's no time."

"How much time?"

"Just over four minutes."

"Until what?" Nero asked.

Asp said, "Four minutes is plenty. Bring your toy inside, Nero. We've already made enough of a mess in here. It won't matter."

"It's across the field. What's the rush?"

"Across the field," Asp repeated. "That's convenient."

"Convenient how?"

"Convenient like finding an unlocked, unguarded police screetbike right where you needed it. Convenient like dodging all them bullets."

"We were all being shot at! It wasn't just me!"

"That neck wound is in the front. The others are in the back."

"Exactly. They shot at me after I got away."

"*After?*" Twilight repeated. "What did they do, detain you?"

"I got away," he told them again.

"So they *did* detain you," Savage said.

"Is there something going on here I'm not aware of?"

"Just wondering how you escaped custody. That's very lucky of you."

Nero began to boil. They weren't taking him seriously. They were treating him the way they'd treat Chase, who was little more than a pickpocket who happened to be smarmy enough to talk his way through smarmy situations.

It wasn't right. Twilight and Asp were unknowns before this, Savage was tough but self-trained, and Daemon hadn't even strapped-on and entered the building, staying safely outside. Only Ryu was more important to or more qualified for this job than Nero. They shouldn't disrespect him like this. He'd surrendered his badge because he believed in ending tech inequity and getting to the bottom of Respero's secrets. And yet they were acting like *he* was the enemy?

"Shut it, everyone," said Ryu. "Strap in. We're about to jump."

They did, trading glances that promised this would be

dealt with later. Nero supposed he understood. He'd been a cop; he could recognize a double-cross. Security at Xenia had been a clusterfuck and their little break-in had clearly been expected. Given the lengths Ryu had gone to ensure their privacy, he doubted that "expectation" had come from a leak. It felt more like a saboteur. It felt more like a snitch, who'd opened his or her mouth to give them away.

That much, Nero understood, because he too kept trying to work out who the rat might be. Problem was, his comrades understood just enough to be annoying. He wanted to punch them until they understood more. Namely, that he wasn't the rat they were looking for. They should look inside — or to the dead — for that.

"Shit," Ryu said.

"What?" Twilight asked.

"No response. The pod won't fire."

"I thought you had it working."

"I did!"

"Working right up until the prodigal son returned," Asp said, staring at Nero.

Asp couldn't possibly mean that Nero had sabotaged the pod. He'd literally just walked in the door. He'd approached in a straight line they'd be able to see if they looked at the hovercam coverage. He'd gone nowhere near any equipment, inside the pod or out. If anyone had sabotaged anything, it was Asp. Or Chase. Or, hell, anyone but him.

"How long?" Ryu asked no one in particular, and that was strange if for no other reason than he was the only one who could answer the question. This was his errand, pod, hacks and software.

"Thirty-three seconds!" Twilight announced.

She was looking at the box in her hands, which Nero

now noticed she was holding like either a baby or a bomb. Her voice was panicked.

"What is that thing?" Nero asked.

"Savage," said Ryu. "Perimeter?"

Savage was checking screens, apparently checking for hostiles. "No contact."

"Twenty-five seconds."

"What are you counting down?" Nero asked Twilight. Then to everyone: "What's happening here?"

Ryu sounded momentarily hopeful, then not so much: "Wait … *shit!*"

"Twenty."

"Maybe it won't happen." Chase was looking up, at a roof with no windows, and out, at curved walls with no windows. "Maybe the first time was a coincidence."

"Fifteen seconds!"

Something clunked — a mechanical sound for a computer-driven situation. It was as if Ryu had, instead of fixing a software bug, moved a rock out from under the pod's wheel, if it had any.

"We're good! Charging!"

"Ten! Nine! FOR WEST'S SAKE HURRY!"

"Jumping!"

The pod dropped. Nero, unprepared, felt his stomach trying to escape skyward. Screens around the place lit as external power came back online, and when they did, Nero saw something that stole his breath, same as everyone's.

That massive black ship from earlier was suddenly above them. He hadn't seen it arrive; the thing seemed to simply appear out of nowhere.

And it was massive. Titanic. Bigger than any hover Nero had seen — more the size of something built in orbit. The screens moved as the pod sensed the direction of the room's attention, shuttling spectrum nanobots from the walls to the roof and finally providing that window Chase had been looking for.

Above, they saw atomized rock in a cloud, not yet reformed. Through the hole, they saw the ship, hovering above the barn, pressing its wooden structure, making the members moan with the squeal of old nails retreating.

The wood began to snap. The ship was descending, an iris on its bottom opening to show red inside.

"Hang on!"

Another downward lurch — Ryu taking them deeper to avoid whatever the ship might be planning from above. The thing hit a cushion of electromagnetic repulsion at its bottom, then lurched forward like a machine suddenly finding its gear. There were G-forces, Ryu pushing the pod faster than it was strictly meant to go.

That made Nero nervous — enough that he was glad the spectrum nanos hadn't given them a forward-facing view. He understood that the pod aerosolized rock so the pod could pass through it, but his nerves ran on emotion rather than intellect.

At this speed, he was sure they'd outrun the forward space created by the engines. They'd go too fast, and hit a rock wall before the pod could reduce it to vapor.

But that didn't happen.

Instead the group's interests must have stayed on the ship, because the pod left a cluster of nanos behind to watch. It didn't pursue. Instead it came straight down, more detonating the barn's superstructure than breaking it apart.

Its fat ass sat on the barn's top, sinking lower until the whole thing gave way. It settled just above the ground, and black-jacketed figures streamed out like ants defending their mound.

Fifteen or twenty ensuing minutes of silence was finally

broken by Ryu. He slowed the pod, then set a sort of autopilot and walked away from the console.

"It didn't follow," he said, meaning the black ship. "We're okay."

"That's because it's not trying to catch us," Nero heard himself say as a new realization dawned. "It's chasing us away."

Chapter Eight

DAEMON

Daemon had already reached that conclusion.

The data supported it, and no other even semi-logical hypotheses.

It was illogical for the box, if the thing could indeed send a ping, to not be constantly sending one. It could call the black ship through solid rock, because they'd been submerged for a long time when the counter first hit zero. If it could summon the ship through rock — and if it wanted them caught — it should be doing so now, rather than letting it remain where they'd recently been.

The box should also have summoned the ship between the last zero and this zero — summoned it right along above them. So why would the box ping *only* at zero, considering the fact that sending pings was an easy thing to do?

It wasn't like the box needed to power up to do it.

It wasn't like it needed an antenna to relay its signal.

Daemon had been watching the telemetry, and was the one person who'd seen the black ship appear this time. He'd never taken his eye from the screens because the data said it would appear at zero and because it had arrived with such rapidity the time before.

So he'd watched, and seen that it had, indeed, *appeared*. It had not flown down from the sky. It had not emerged from a structure and pulled up like a hover on the street. No, the entire bulwark had simply popped into existence.

Daemon knew of nothing that could explain it — nothing but the simple explanation that turned out in the end to be true.

Even the ideas of *de novo* materialization or some sort of teleportation didn't hold water. Daemon had explored those ideas in the past, of course, because he explored and investigated anything that ran on electrons and zero-point energy.

Even if Xenia or Quark *had* developed the ability to teleport objects (some of that secret tech they wished to spill into the world), those technologies would have left traces or shown energetic footprints that the black ship did not.

Daemon supposed it was possible that teleportation tech existed and employed a technology foreign to him (one that didn't leave traces), but he doubted it. In science as in life, Occam's razor applied: *The simplest answer was almost always the true one.*

The ship's arrival (and its identity; Daemon had theories about that as well) weren't really the most pertinent questions. Practicality mattered. So many people got hung up on the *why* of things, when the *what* mattered infinitely more.

The *what* in this case was the ship's function, not its nature or the mode of its conveyance. It was much more important to put limited brain space on that issue rather than the *why* of it all.

Daemon was the perfect man to figure it out, because

he had a partition installed in his brain. It was like an internal firewall. Metaphorically speaking, it was as if the human mind was a giant clockwork machine in which a person's personality lived, like an operator pulling levers.

In most people, personality (ego, if you will) ran things. But not so in Daemon. The firewall had separated his *self* from the machinery of his mind, then locked that self in a small corner. He still had a personality, of course, but its sloppy emotion and dull human concerns no longer interfered with the smooth running of the machine.

The machine, in turn, had been augmented by a few Quark add-ons since the firewalling gave it so much extra space in which to spread out. Ryu, in payment for Daemon's participation in this job, had de-throttled his mind using those add-ons.

One such implant was a statistical calculator. Another was a redundant memory cache that gave Daemon perfect recall of the past twenty-four hours. He had an optical port, of course, and a dashboard projector. He carried a protected, duplicated dataset from the most relevant sections of The Beam, updated live when he was connected and predictive when he was not.

It all made Daemon very smart — smart and logical like a robot. Few people could really relate to him these days, but that was fine. His analyses — and his anticipations — were all excellent.

Using that superior analysis, he'd decided that the black ship wasn't what it appeared. He wasn't dumb enough to say it out loud, though — as was immediately proven when Nero said the same thing.

"What makes you say that?" Asp asked him, getting up and limping over.

Daemon averted his eyes; he'd lost most of his subtle social cues when he'd made room for all that processing power. If anyone so much as looked his way, it'd be clear just how much he had figured out. He hadn't revealed any of it because there were still pieces missing from the logic puzzle. Namely, the fact that someone in the group had leaked their plan, either intentionally or by accident.

Until Daemon knew who it was, speaking up would only ruin the solution matrix he'd been working out inside his mind. It would also make him a target, because *there's a traitor among us* was the one thing pretty much everyone in the pod had figured out ... and those who knew the most became the likeliest suspects.

Nero explained his thinking about the black ship as the others watched him.

His logic was much like Daemon's. He'd seen the ship while running around on his screetbike, then again just now. He had a cop's mind, and the extensive personal and service record Daemon had hacked up painted Nero as extremely introspective, extremely logical ... basically extremely good at the job of solving crimes.

Of course he had deduced the same thing as Daemon.

If the ship wanted to *get* them instead of just follow and annoy them, it would be chasing a constant live ping from the box. Not one that happened every six hours and thirty-three minutes.

There was something else that only Daemon and Ryu knew and didn't yet plan to tell the others for fear of what it might mean. The ping couldn't be blocked. The box wasn't really even *pinging*, technically speaking — not in any way he understood. They'd put it inside a Faraday cage while studying it, using the same signal-blocking protocol Ryu used everywhere. But the cage barred nothing.

Analytics showed data streaming into that strange, motionless block of whatever-it-was despite the cage, and they showed data moving out. The thing acted, in short, like it was connected to The Beam.

And yet it managed to do so without a physical connection, without electromagnetic signals on any wavelength at all. Its power source seemed dodgy as well. The box wasn't powered by any battery Daemon was familiar with, and received no inductive power.

That all made Daemon wonder just what in the world it really was. Other than one *hell* of a codebreaker. He had walked outside of the thing's seeming range to test it. Though its range, too, seemed to change depending on the box's wishes — if he anthropomorphized it — and composed a new code using the longest encryption keys he'd ever seen: 4.096 kilobit indices entangled in a set of quantum-paired particles from a miniature hypermagnetic accelerator of his own design.

Daemon hadn't measured the particles' position or momentum, so the Uncertainty Principle would apply like a motherfucker. The result was a randomly generated code with no semantic match, so the decoded message couldn't even be guessed at. He'd encoded it using means nobody, including himself, would ever be able to deduce ... but none of that had been a problem for the box.

The code unraveled itself the second Daemon brought the tablet close, easy as pie. He only knew its cleartext was right because he'd left metadata fingerprints all over the thing, and the metadata showed Daemon as creator. It wasn't like he had any clue how to solve the puzzle otherwise. Only the box was sure.

Impressive.

But also a total unknown. The more Daemon thought about the box, the more he felt like a caveman trying to understand a Bell telephone. The tech was easy enough even for the first phone users, but beyond the caveman's ability to remotely understand. It wasn't that the caveman was dumb. Not that the caveman simply needed to be educated, even. No, *the very concept itself* was twenty layers past the caveman.

To understand the transmission of sound, you had to understand vibrational waves in compressed air. You had to understand electronic conduction — and to understand *that*, you had to know about electrons. About atoms. About the existence of wire, to go back a step.

It was hard to blame a caveman for thinking the source of the phone's voice was inside the phone itself. That was the world he knew. Those were the assumptions he based his life upon. The way Daemon trusted that gravity would keep working, *that's* how firmly the caveman's beliefs would be rooted.

Right now, Daemon was a caveman before that box. He didn't understand the thing, and neither did Ryu. Worse, they didn't even understand what they needed to understand to understand it … and they didn't understand what they needed to understand *that*.

Ryu said, *Don't tell the others it's impossible to understand. Let them think it's just something we need to work out.*

Fine with Daemon, because he doubted it *could* be worked out, at all, ever. He didn't need to tell anyone just how deep the box was down the rabbit hole because nobody other than Daemon or Ryu would ever try to dig.

If Daemon had still been capable of fear, the box would have terrified him. Because as impossible as it sounded, Ryu said the box appeared to know even more than The Beam.

It did things The Beam couldn't do. Maybe it was just more of that advanced Xenia tech they wanted to loose upon the world, but Ryu didn't think so and Daemon agreed. The box didn't just *seem* to be above The Beam;

the box *was* above The Beam. In order to create the box, a *person* would need to be above The Beam.

But what on earth was above the network that ran everything?

"Look …" Nero swallowed. At some point while Daemon was cogitating, the other five, standing, had encircled Nero, sitting. "I just get this feeling."

"What feeling?" Twilight asked.

"That we're being fucked with."

"Yeah." Asp stared hard at Nero. "I wonder *who* could possibly be fucking with us?"

Nero stood and faced him. "Is there something you want to say, Gerard?"

"Fuck you," Asp replied.

"Wait." Chase turned to Mr. Cool. "Your real name is *Gerard?*"

"Knock it off," Ryu said. "No real names."

"Wait," said Savage, looking at the pair of facing men. "Do you two know each other?"

"No." Asp shook his head. "I'm just really good at guessing."

Savage turned to Ryu. "You said nobody knew each other."

"Almost nobody," he replied without apology.

"That's not what you said."

"It's handled. I vouch for everyone here." Again, no apology.

"Good vouching," said Asp, turning on Ryu.

"We agreed," Savage went on. "Total anonymity."

"That's what I delivered," Ryu told her.

"Tell that to Blaine and Gerard."

"How's it matter?"

"Because it wasn't true. What else isn't true, Ryu?"

"Nothing."

"We never checked on what Tenor was talking about," Savage said, moving her gaze between Asp, Nero, and Ryu. "Probably take three full-grown men to install a covert antenna and enough shielding to hide it."

"Bullshit."

Twilight: "Let's just calm down."

Chase: "Asp was last out of the building."

"I was shot!"

"And so was Nero," Chase argued. "Pretty good way to deflect suspicion."

Asp turned to him. "Let me get this straight. You're saying we got ourselves shot because we're in cahoots with Xenia."

"*And* apparently in cahoots with each other," Nero added, also turning toward Chase.

Savage put a hand on Asp's shoulder to turn him around. Not a good move. He spun fast despite his injury, slapping her hand away and then shoving her in the chest.

"Don't you touch me."

"You didn't say you knew Nero," Savage said, undaunted.

"You didn't ask."

"What else didn't you tell us?"

"I was born without a butthole. They had to cut it open. I don't like Starbucks. I never fold my shorts. What else do you want to know?"

"How do you know him?"

"We were in the same knitting circle."

"I'm serious."

"So am I."

"OKAY, KNOCK IT OFF!"

Ryu's shout stopped everyone.

Tempers were climbing, but they were all wanted now, and wanted by forces they didn't understand. Ryu had gotten them into this, and only he could get them out of it. Daemon's observation and deductions said that some of them suspected him. But they'd still follow him in the end, because right now there were no other options.

"It's true. Asp and Nero both worked on a job with me before." Ryu glared at them both; apparently this was a secret they'd agreed to keep. "It was years ago and there were no problems with the job. I wanted a crew without any history, but Asp and Nero were the best I knew, and there was no reason to risk the mission by going with lesser people just to ensure a totally clean slate. I should have said something, but I honestly didn't think it would come up. So there it is. Now you know."

"What else don't we know?" Savage asked.

"Nothing."

"And we're just supposed to trust you?"

"Stop," Daemon said.

Everyone looked. He usually only spoke when someone addressed him. His single quiet word was as effective an argument-breaker as Ryu's full-on shout.

When a dozen eyes turned to him, Daemon felt himself wanting to retreat. He didn't like attention and already wished that he hadn't invited it.

"I've run all scenarios. The only ones with any remaining chance of success require what remains of this unit to stay intact."

He could put it more bluntly, but that felt a bridge too far. Daemon *had* run all the scenarios, and the bigger truth was that all of the success scenarios wouldn't just require all of them in order to work; they were also extremely unlikely.

The job was an off-balance wheel and was growing increasingly hard to stabilize. That wheel had begun to wobble when Xenia went bad, wobbled more when they'd lost two people on-site, then began to rattle off its bearings when two of the survivors had attempted mutiny and died in front of everyone.

The chances of righting that failing wheel were, in Daemon's mind, minuscule. His conclusion was simple and grim: *If they kept arguing, then everyone would die.*

With the box as play maker, the game felt rigged. Everyone was acting like it wasn't part of this, but in Daemon's estimation the box was everything.

"We didn't know what we were getting into, but we're into it now. There's good news and bad news, as far as I can tell."

Even Ryu waited anxiously.

Daemon continued. "The good news is that I think what Nero said is true. The people who were at Xenia — the people behind that black ship — could easily catch and kill us."

"That really is good news," Twilight said. "Thanks a lot."

"The fact that they haven't means they probably don't want to." He buried the *at least not yet* part before it left his lips out loud.

"What's the bad news?" Chase asked.

"It has something to do with the box."

They all looked at the thing. Someone had put it on a chair, as if the box was having a rest.

"What makes you say that?"

"They let us take it. Maybe they even wanted us to."

"Good enough," said Twilight. "Let's give it back."

"We're not giving it back." Savage shook her head. "You've seen what that thing can do."

"Exactly. I've seen what it can do."

"What are you afraid of, Twilight? It hasn't done anything dangerous."

"Except stall the pod. Except call the black ship."

"To follow us," Nero suggested. "Maybe to drive us somewhere."

"Where?" Asp asked.

"It doesn't matter. We have to keep the box." Daemon couldn't explain the rest, but he felt sure it was true. Some of the data wafting off the box like strange heat looked akin to quantum computing to him — and no amateur's version, either.

That might mean the box was making mathematical predictions, possibly even about the near-term future. Free will didn't matter as much as people liked to pretend; Daemon had seen that first-hand after having his partition installed.

He'd lived over sixty years as a human obsessed with self-determination, then discovered after logic descended that it'd all been an illusion anyway. With enough present-moment data, predicting the near future wasn't even difficult. The expression went, Garbage In, Garbage Out — GIGO in early computing terms.

The inverse was also true. Daemon didn't think the box was as mute and dull and inert as it appeared. He thought, conversely, that it was probably the smartest one here. The box knowing what would happen next proved that free will was just an illusion.

They had to keep the box because in non-linear terms, they'd sort of *already* kept it. Destiny was as apt a way to label their situation as anything.

"Why?"

"Because if we get rid of the box, the wrong people will end up with it. And then the wrong things will happen."

"What things?"

"I don't know."

"Oh, for fuck's sake," said Asp.

"What makes you so sure?" Twilight asked.

Daemon shrugged. "*I* just know that *it* knows."

They all looked at the box. Daemon assumed they were all thinking the same thing: *Was this true? Were they really stuck with it?*

Every mind around him was running possibilities. They knew the box counted down, but not really what it did each time it hit zero.

They knew it called the ship, but must be starting to see that the ship in itself wasn't really a threat … for now.

They didn't know that each countdown resulted in a frenetic burst of code-eating, though — a sign that somewhere, somehow, encryption was being opened wide every time the countdown expired.

What exactly the box was decoding, Daemon had no clue. But even if they'd known, the group probably wasn't yet afraid of it because calling a nonsense ship and decoding mysteries weren't obvious threats. At least not immediately.

That meant they were actually trying to justify ways to keep the box. If they kept it, they'd be able to complete the moral and social mission that Savage was so hot to complete. There would be secrets they could sell, earning the payday they'd gotten into this for in the first place.

Right now, all six other people in the room were telling themselves it was safe. Everything was fine. They could still do this, and it would all work out according to their extremely meticulous plan.

Daemon felt otherwise, because of that quantum-computing, predicting-the-future thing. It wasn't that he wanted to get rid of the box. It was more that he knew the decision was already made in a cosmic sense, and that there was nothing anyone could do to change it.

More importantly, though, Daemon was increasingly certain that they hadn't really found the box. It had found them, for reasons of its own (or those of its creator).

If the box had the power Daemon was thinking it did, then the thing would not be dissuaded from those reasons so easily. If they tried to silence its transmissions to unknown parties, they'd fail. If they tried to destroy it, there would be consequences. If they dropped it by the roadside, Daemon suspected the box would find its way back.

They were germs in the gut of an enormous creature. Any illusions that they could change their fates were just that: *illusions*.

"Daemon, Ryu," said Twilight, looking at the box with new respect, tinged with nerves, "what *is* that thing?"

But neither of them could answer.

Nor could anyone else.

Chapter Nine

CHASE

THERE WAS a knock at the door. Chase didn't have his own room in the pod — nobody did — but there were a few small spaces that had been converted for use behind closed doors and it was unanimously agreed that the one behind the conduit mains belonged exclusively to him.

Simple triage. Chase spent most of his time harassing the others, particularly the women. Everyone seemed to have decided he was a pig, and that the less time hogs like him spent outside of closed doors, the better. Chase also knew that everyone let him have the room because they assumed he spent most of his time inside masturbating. It was true. Nobody wanted to bunk up with that.

In truth, Chase didn't find Twilight or Savage remotely sexy. He wasn't interested in either and definitely wasn't wasting any masturbation time on them. Same for Smoke, before she'd bought it.

Smoke was old, Twilight was whiny, and Savage probably fucked like a mantis, devouring her mate afterward. More importantly, though, they all had vaginas. Chase wasn't interested in vaginas — those vile, bread-making things. He would have come out long ago, but for some reason the criminal world was the last real bastion of homophobia left in the NAU.

Chase didn't even understand that. If breaking the law took balls, what had more balls than a pair of men?

"Chase?" said the low voice outside.

"Come in."

Nero entered. He sat beside Chase and they kissed, but it was a halfway thing.

"What?" Nero asked.

Chase reached to the side of the cot. He came up with the codebreaker box.

"Why do you have that?"

"Everyone's asleep. It was just sitting out there."

Nero looked at the wall-mounted clock. With their Beam blackout, it was an ancient round thing — Ryu had had to teach Chase how to tell time. He followed Nero's gaze to see it was after midnight.

"Were you waiting for me?" Nero scooted closer, but Chase flinched away. "What the hell's the matter with you?"

Instead of answering, Chase slid his hands along the box. The display lit.

"Not long," Nero said, looking at the thing.

"I'm talking about the other line." The one that read, ITERATION 5 OF 11.

"Huh," said Nero.

"That's your response? You don't think it's strange?"

Nero shrugged. "Ryu said he doesn't know what the iterations mean."

"Twilight thinks it's counting deaths."

Nero laughed. "You don't think that, do you?"

"Why not?"

"For starters, only four people have died."

"I know." Chase nodded. "It said two when two were dead. Then it said four after Tenor and Locus bit it."

"But now it says five."

"Okay."

"So what if five are dead?"

Nero looked at Chase for a long time without speaking.

Chase shook his head. Almost nobody saw him in his natural form like this. Only former lovers, then Nero. The others hated him because he was a loud, womanizing chauvinist. He was actually none of those things, but it paid to project a certain image in his rather aggressive line of work.

"I keep thinking about what you said about when they caught you."

"What about it?" Nero asked.

"When the Clerics caught you."

Now he must've seen the edge of what Chase was saying. Shifting, he said, "Yeah."

"What did they look like? The Clerics?"

"You've never seen one?"

Chase shook his head. Few people had. A lot of people thought they were only a rumor. The idea of nanobots operating human bodies like puppets sounded like something from a paranoid fantasy. They were semi-normal to Nero, because most of Quark's proprietary police force were Clerics. He'd heard they even had their own wing at DZPD now, acting like actual cops.

"They look like people," Nero answered.

"How much like people?"

"Identical. You'd never know. Except they have …"

"What?"

"Flies in their eyes."

"What's that mean?"

Nero explained, trying and failing to put a hand on

Chase's leg. He was too keyed up for affection. Paranoia wasn't typically part of his nature, but today had been that kind of day. First they'd entered a heist that seemed changed just before they arrived, stocked with pursuers who were strange at best — pursuers who Nero's account to the others claimed were Beam Clerics.

Then two of their number had mutinied and died, followed by a series of increasingly suspicious arguments, and a sneaking suspicion that Daemon's predictions about their future were actually far more grim than the weirdo was letting on. It was becoming hard to know what and *who* to believe.

"That's how you tell them from people? You can spot the flies in their eyes?"

"Usually. That's how I knew the ones who got me were Clerics."

"But not always?"

"Apparently they can go dormant," Nero said. "Hide in the brain and spinal column and let biology take over."

"So there's no way to tell?"

"Sure there is. You could cut them open."

Chase laughed, but a second later he flicked open the knife he'd been holding beside his leg and pressed the tip to Nero's gut.

"Whoa." Nero laughed to show Chase he knew this was a poorly placed joke, but he was also smart enough to know that it absolutely was not. "What's going on here?"

"How did you get away?"

"I got one of their guns and stole a screetbike, exactly like I told you."

"And the bike was just sitting there."

Nero's hands had gone up. Chase didn't remember them actually rising. "Yeah."

"Liar."

"Now wait just a fucking—"

Chase pressed the tip harder against his shirt. The blade was sharp. One quick thrust and this would be over.

"Chase," Nero said.

"Prove you're him."

"What?"

"Prove you're not a Cleric."

"*What?*"

"You heard me. Ryu admitted we'd never know. He said he'd never even thought there might be Clerics. And that was good, because it's not like he can scan for them. They're human bodies, right? One could walk right up to us and none of the alarms would go off."

"That … Chase. Put the knife down. It's me."

Another push of the knife. "I said prove it."

Patiently, Nero said, "That's not how it works. They're manufactured that way. They clone human tissue, but bypass normal nervous system development and substitute nanobots to do the thinking and controlling. Cleric bodies are born as meat puppets. They can't … *possess* people."

"Clones," Chase repeated.

"What?"

"You said they're human clones."

"I said they clone human tissue. From stock cell lines. And it has to grow over time. You can't seriously think—"

"I think someone ratted us out," Chase said, not letting Nero finish. "I think Ryu's AI surveillance is thorough, and would have detected anyone speaking a message or sending one with a tablet or mobile or canvas terminal. Put those together and there's really only one way a person could send a message." He stopped. "Well. Not a *person.*"

"You think I'm a Cleric? You know me!"

"Yeah. Maybe you've always been a Cleric. That story you told me? About Captain Dominic Long and the sister he hid from federal Respero? I had a friend look into your little fairy tale a few weeks ago. He said something like that would be extremely hard to pull off. Long would probably have needed help from someone inside."

"Inside what?"

"You tell me. Maybe from inside The Beam."

Nero straightened. "Okay. Tell me how you want me to prove I'm human and I'll do it. I'm the same person I always was, Chase. Nothing's changed."

Chase wasn't so sure. All he knew about Beam Clerics had come from Nero, including that little tidbit about how they were manufactured as Clerics and couldn't jump from host to host — or clone full-sized hosts to replace the original.

The latter didn't seem farfetched at all. Nanobots were used for spinal cord injuries too dangerous to operate on, injected and instructed to camp on motor neurons and musculature so they could animate dead limbs manually. That sounded like puppetry to Chase, same as NPS swarm nanos could paralyze a suspect, same as Ryu had nanos that could turn off a person's eyes so he could speak to them without being seen.

How farfetched was it, really, that nanos could take over an entire body — even a brain, if anything he'd heard about Project Mindbender held water.

What's more, how farfetched was it that Nero, if he knew those things were possible, would lie about it if he was one of them?

"The box says five people are dead."

"Obviously that's not what the box is saying, because nobody else has died."

"Unless the real Nero has."

Nero seemed to realize just how serious this was. "You're not being logical."

"How long have you known Asp?"

"What's that got to do with anything?"

"You never told me you knew him."

"I didn't think it mattered."

"You ever fuck him?"

"*What?*"

"You heard me. *Asp.*"

"Asp is straight."

"Everyone thinks *we're* straight."

"I barely even—"

"Just like everyone thought Rogue was straight."

Nero froze. Chase could almost hear his mind spinning, trying to find a way out of this. But there was no way out, unless that way was *through*.

He knew too much. Secrets right now kept getting easier and easier to find.

"How did you find out?" Nero asked.

"Your backups. They're on the server." Chase nodded to the screen at the foot of his co-opted bed. They all synced with the pod's server for security reasons. With no outgoing or incoming signals, all they had to coordinate the mission was coherence between the actions of the people involved.

"But they're …" Nero stopped.

"Encrypted?" Chase finished. "Yeah. They were. But after we left the barn, I checked some of my own files, and there *your* files were, suddenly unlocked."

"After the barn?"

"Yeah."

"After the box hit zero?"

"This isn't about the box."

"Listen to me, Chase. I keep thinking about this, and I think the box might be—"

The blade broke through Nero's shirt and nicked his skin.

"How long?" Chase asked.

"How long what?"

"Don't fucking insult me. Don't you dare."

Nero nodded as if he understood. "I knew Rogue, too. Since years ago."

"And you were lovers."

"Not then."

"When?"

"It was recent. When the job started."

"So right around the time we hooked up. Look at you. Eight men on the job and three in the closet. What are the odds? Unless you planned it that way."

"What are you talking about?"

Chase attempted to marshal his thoughts. He'd been cycling for hours now, thinking in near silence since the rest of the pod had bedded down early, trying to rest before the big black ship returned.

He'd been hurt and angry upon finding the videos Nero had taken of himself with Rogue. He'd wanted to understand, and had spent the time since cobbling a possible explanation together. But the more he thought about it, the surer he became.

This wasn't really Ryu's mission.

Ryu thought it was, but Nero was really pulling the strings. Nero had known two of the supposedly unknown members for years and he'd formed an immediate alliance with a third: Chase. All of them were wanted by NPS, but Ryu most of all.

Chase figured this was really all about setting a trap for Ryu. They wanted his network and various hideouts instead of just the man himself, so they'd crafted a plan that was bound to fail, then planted a tracker.

What else made sense? What else explained how Nero had been caught … then escaped … on a bike that had been so conveniently left for him to find?

"What does the box do?" Chase asked.

"I don't know! Chase, I'm not—"

"Did I ever even *meet* the real Nero? Or have I only met his Cleric clone?"

"I'm not a Cleric!"

"Prove it."

"I can't prove it without—"

"Get up."

Nero stood as Chase continued to poke.

"Open the door."

"Let's talk about this. You have a right to be angry. But just because I didn't tell you the truth about Rogue—"

"Or Asp."

"—or Asp, that doesn't mean I—"

"Open the door!"

Nero followed the order. Chase poked him out into the main area of the pod, reaching back as an afterthought to take the black cube under his arm.

Twilight stirred on one of the public-area bunks. She rubbed her eyes, then quickly stood. "Whoa. Chase. What's … What's up?"

Ryu lifted his head. "What's going on?"

Chase, now the center of swelling attention, realized he hadn't thought far enough ahead. He was the righteous one here, but since he hadn't bothered to pre-present his case to the others, now he looked like the crazy one.

"He's a Cleric," Chase said.

"What?" Ryu looked either incredulous or confused.

"I'm not a Cleric."

"The people who grabbed him were Clerics. They let him go. It's the only explanation."

"Now, hang on," Ryu said, standing with arms up, palms out.

"They took him over. Took over the real Nero." That wasn't right, though. His nerves were getting the best of him. He wasn't completely sure the real Nero was still out there (or dead; the box said he was dead), but he was *pretty* sure, and it felt right. He only knew that this man was a liar. This man was a traitor. This man had broken his heart.

"That's not how it works with Clerics," Ryu told him.

Then Chase realized. "You're in on it."

"Put the knife down." Savage was circling, trying to get close enough to grab him.

But Chase was smarter than that. He put his back toward the empty wall, flashed the blade at Savage, and waved the rest of them away. "Of course. Now it all makes sense."

"What makes sense?" said Asp.

"All of it. Ryu and Nero know all about the clerics. They didn't screen for them. They—"

"You *can't* screen for them!" Ryu exclaimed. "It's not necessary. Inside a dampening field like the one around the pod, signals can't get in or out. Clerics can only operate for so long without access to The Beam."

"Uh-huh," said Chase. "And who designed the dampening field? *You?*"

"You're out of line," Savage told him.

"I guess you're in on it too, then."

Savage looked offended — not at the insult, but at Chase's piss-poor logic. She half-smirked. "Is that how this is going to go? Anyone who disagrees with you is part of some conspiracy? Put down the fucking knife and stop being an idiot!"

Shit. This was already sideways. Everyone was up and

out now, and all of them were eyeing him like a hostage-holder. He hadn't planned it that way; this was just always how his attempts to make a stand came out. He'd planned to keep Nero under control while calmly explaining his theory to the others, then letting Ryu or Daemon take all the time they wanted to untangle the truth.

Instead he now had Nero with an arm around the throat, hiding behind him with the knife to his back. Nero's hands were still up, making things look worse. Despite his best intentions, Chase's arguments had him sounding like a lunatic.

"Stay back. Don't get near me."

They might not have meant to corner him, but it was happening anyway. The pod was only so big, and it wasn't like he could just hop out a window. They were still moving, cutting a wide loop back toward District Zero's imposing skyline through solid rock. Ryu said he needed time to think, to work out what all of this meant.

Ryu was stalling. Adjusting so he could maintain control of this nefarious plan.

"If you come any closer, I'll kill him." Chase was nearly against the wall now. There was just the alcove behind him, the door to the outside.

His heart leapt when he brushed the hatch lever, irrationally certain it would open and he'd tumble outside. That couldn't happen while the pod was buried, but his nerves were on fire, his brain not thinking right.

"Nobody has to get hurt," said Ryu, taking the lead. "Why don't you just tell us what happened to start all of this."

"He fucked Rogue." The truth left his mouth accidentally. The statement outed all three of them and had no relevance to the situation at hand, but his mind was Jell-O. This was the verbal version of panic fire.

Savage was coming closer, moving slowly with her arms at her sides.

But Chase knew she was thinking. She'd come at him soon, Ryu or no Ryu.

"I said stay back," Chase said directly to Savage.

"You won't hurt him," she said.

"Savage," Ryu said, "back off."

But her eyes were smiling. She hated Chase. Hated him and Tenor with a passion. Maybe she was even the reason Tenor was dead, if Savage was in on the scam the way Nero and Ryu apparently were.

She didn't back off or even slow. Savage thought she knew something better than Chase, that righteous bitch. With her moral reason for pulling this job — thinking she was better than him, seeing as he was in this for the money.

Well, fuck her.

"I'll do it," Chase said.

"Then what? What exactly do you think will happen if you kill Nero? We'll just shake your hand and say, 'Hey, everyone makes mistakes'?"

"I mean it, Savage."

"But it won't get that far, will it? You won't hurt Nero. You love him."

"What?" said Asp.

"I know a love triangle when I see one. I knew about Rogue. He wasn't really that far in the closet. It's almost the twenty-second century, boys. You should be more enlightened."

"Wait …" Asp was only now getting it. "You mean all three of them are—?"

"But I figured it was Tenor," Savage said, still nearing them with the twining approach of a serpent. "Tenor was the one who tried to drag Rogue out of there. He acted just as closeted as you. Just as afraid of who he really was."

"I'M WARNING YOU, BACK OFF!"

There was shouting.

Many people moved at once, in different directions.

The air filled with alarmed sounds and protests: many entreaties like *Stop!* and *No!* and *Look out!*

Because the pod door had opened behind Chase. His brainstem knew it before his prefrontal cortex; he could feel the hot *whoosh* of liquid rock to his rear.

It happened only after Savage made her move — after she was committed.

The whole affair happened one-two-three.

One: Savage rushing Chase and Nero, sure Chase was bluffing, determined to disarm him and end this facade.

Two: The pod door opening even though it was sealed, seated tight by physics and software. Nothing should have been able to open it.

Three: Savage striking them both like a football tackle, sending all three people not against the door as planned, but out into the cloud of atomized earth instead.

Then silence.

Except when the box lit its own display, dropped by Chase as he retreated.

It made a clicking sound, as if clucking its tongue to nab their attention.

It read, ITERATION 7 OF 11.

With five minutes to go.

Chapter Ten

ROGUE

SEVEN MONTHS EARLIER

THE BAG WAS PULLED from Mitchell Ordner's head, and he found himself in a familiar-sounding warehouse.

He could hear machinery and birds in the distance, plus the low purr of a light breeze rattling unknown parts, like a huge corrugated-metal door Mitchell knew was a little loose behind its rider wheels.

The entire building was manual. Blocks and tackles for raising cargo instead of engines, loud wheeled dollies for pushing wood and I-beams about instead of letting a few simple hoverbots do the job. It was ironic: Ryu was perhaps the best technologist in District Zero's underground, but his hallmark was an austere lack of technology. He lived more like a technophobe than the Organa, who always cheated a bit here and there. Ryu never cheated. He was either so immersed that he saw the world in lines of code, or backwards enough to have written *Walden*.

It was an occupational hazard mixed with a dose of paranoia just large enough to keep him alive. No machines or software meant nothing to hack. It was like saving a gangrenous arm by simply cutting it off.

"I still can't see anything," Mitchell said.

Something tapped his temple. He looked up to find Ryu holding his small can of specialty nanobots. The can never opened, and the nanos moved in and out through holes too small for any sort of view.

"Better?"

Mitchell nodded. "One or the other would do. Bag or nanobots, not both."

"I like to be safe. Usually I wear a mask. I still don't let them see me."

"So this is an advantage I have? Being 'allowed' to see your ugly mug?"

They paused, laughed, then embraced.

Ryu didn't laugh much, but the two of them went way back. That didn't mean he got to know where the mysterious man (really, a ghost) lived or worked, but then again nobody was trusted enough for that.

"What do you have for me?" Ryu asked.

"Do you mean the Stark suit?"

"The suit is for you. *Rogue*."

"How about 'Mitch'?"

"I prefer codenames that aren't incredibly obvious."

"I was kidding."

"I know."

"'Ordner' is better."

"Please," Ryu said, waving a hand. "Sit."

Once inside, Mitchell was always impressed with Ryu's private spaces. For someone so austere, he lived well. Not extravagantly, but he was a man with taste who knew how to use it. And for such a wanted man, Ryu had a way of putting the people he liked at ease. There weren't many.

"About the suit," Mitchell said.

"We need the suit," Ryu said, anticipating the objection. Technically Mitchell could get a Stark Centurion suit, and technically Mitchell had access enough at Xenia to make that suit MIA from inventory. Technically, they weren't going to get caught appropriating such an expensive and confidential piece of paramilitary equipment, but also technically, taking it gave Mitchell the shakes. He knew what the suits had been designed for. He knew what they could do.

"Why?"

"For the job. We need you, in the suit, taking lead."

"It's not armor. Those suits are actually pretty susceptible to—"

"I get it. I know. But they'll deflect any weapon we'll encounter and it's important to sow doubt. This can't look like a break-in by terrorists. We can't deflect surveillance, so at the very least DZPD is going to have footage of all we do during the heist … and at most, they'll leak it to the press."

"And?"

"It needs to look like an inside job. Our spin is that insiders at Xenia saw things they couldn't stomach. That makes us heroes who refused to turn a blind eye rather than vandals."

"And you don't think there's a more subtle way to do that than wearing a Stark suit?"

"It's not just the public who I intend to send a message," Ryu said.

Mitchell thought about that. He'd known Ryu since they were in school together, but Ryu had never fully opened up. Ryu — who back then had been called Timothy — was always a man with secret plans. *Layers* of secret plans. Mitchell was never entirely sure that he was in on the real plan when they worked together, or even just when they talked. He always felt like a pawn in some larger game. That was probably more true of the forthcoming Xenia heist than anything else.

It's not just the public who I intend to send a message.

Cryptic, but Mitchell was still pretty sure he knew what Ryu meant. Rumor said it was Ryan Industries who'd spearheaded the Stark Centurion program, and Ryan Industries was the Beau Monde at its zenith.

There might even be a secret societal tier above Beau Monde, inhabited disproportionately by the Ryan family. Rachel, for instance. She was nearly 150 years old, practically a Cleric herself for all the nano treatments she'd had to keep her skin sack from falling apart. Rachel and the mafia, the mafia and Rachel. That's who Ryu wanted to see in those surveillance feeds. That's to whom Ryu meant to send a message.

We got you, asshole. We know what you built, we used it against you, and soon the world will have it all.

"It's just that a suit like that—"

"Don't, Rogue," said Ryu. "You're the only one who can pilot it. You said you want to help on the ground. This is how you help. If you want out, I won't be offended. We can do this without showing them that we got at one of their goddamn war suits, but the breach is what matters."

"I want to help on the ground."

There were practical reasons for that. Ryu claimed that nobody would ever know it was Mitchell who'd betrayed Xenia, and he knew Ryu well enough to believe it. But Mitchell himself was the problem. He couldn't go to work the next day with a neutral face. His first word about the break-in would give him away. He wanted to help Ryu's team in actual action — not just intel — because his team would have to go underground once it was over.

It mattered to few of them: Ryu, for one, had spent

his adult life underground. Mitchell knew that if he let Ryu and the others into the lab, it was the end of Mitchell Ordner and the true beginning of alter-ego Rogue. It was fine. He had no family, few friends, and couldn't stomach what Xenia was doing for even one more workday.

He could become a revolutionary. He could vanish.

This was his way to do it clean.

Ryu nodded in a *Well, that's settled* sort of way. He sat with one leg crossed over the other.

"Okay," Mitchell said. "I guess you want to see it."

Ryu nodded slowly.

Mitchell opened a portable terminal. It was obsolete, as Ryu required within his bubble of no-tech. It was *so* obsolete, in fact, that Mitchell had needed to rescue it from recycling.

They'd destroy it after this little demonstration, but it was a shame. The thing wasn't just old; it felt like a piece of history. An original prototype, circa 2060 — one of the first portable canvases to access The Beam, back before Crossbrace had fully evolved into the heaven and hell the world had now.

"Canvas," Mitchell said.

"Hello, Mitchell," the featureless gray laptop replied in a female voice.

A woman appeared ten feet away. She was brunette, well-dressed, standing upright but not artificially so.

"Who is that?" Ryu asked.

"My ex-wife."

"You were married?"

"I wanted kids."

"To a woman?"

"I'm flexible. It was faster than adoption. Do you want her off?"

Ryu shook his head. "I actually like holography for things like this. I'm just surprised."

"That it's a woman."

"That anyone would have an ex for their avatar."

"You get that I didn't choose her."

"Oh, I know. It's so much more revealing that the canvas chose her for you."

"The default is Noah West. I can change it."

Ryu shook his head. "Not on the prototypes. They only started making West the default after the avatar program started creeping people out."

"I think I know our tech better than you, Ryu."

"If you say so."

Annoyed, Mitchell called up a holo web and began to scrub through it for the avatar settings. But of course Ryu was right; he only had the option of this avatar or no avatar at all.

Ryu didn't gloat. He just waited for the delay to be over.

"Canvas."

"Yes, Mitchell."

"Show us the inventory I loaded this morning."

"Of course, Mitchell."

Rather than projecting onto one of Ryu's existing tables, the canvas created its own holographic table to hold Mitchell's holographic flea market. He looked over to see if Ryu was impressed. He didn't seem to be. A shame because Mitchell certainly was. The portable canvas was almost forty years old, and yet it projected holograms that looked like solid matter.

"Begin tour."

The holographic woman picked up the first of the holographic objects. A small can similar to the one Ryu used to hold his blackout nanobots.

"Nanos?"

Mitchell nodded. "Series Six."

"Canvas. Enlarge on that reservoir's contents."

The early canvas wouldn't be fully intuitive unless it was connected to The Beam, and Mitchell knew better than to do that — not when he found the mothballed thing and certainly not now. It was intuitive enough, though. From the beginning, Beam AI had been nearly as human. It didn't just zoom in on the can or show a smattering of tiny dots. It knew Ryu wanted to see the nanos up close, so that's what the next hologram showed him.

"What's the scale?"

"Two hundred nanometers."

"So the actual bot is …"

"Specs are about seventy nanometers across the longest dimension."

"Small."

"They go smaller."

"How?"

"Micro atomics. Don't ask. I don't know how it works."

Ryu examined the holo, standing up to circle it. "This has moving parts. Real moving parts."

"Micro atomics," Mitchell repeated.

"What are they spec'd for?"

"Clarissa?" Mitchell asked the hologram.

"Yes, Mitchell." Then to Ryu. "Designated catalog specifications, Xenia Labs, Inc, calls for recreational or military applications."

"Explain."

"Series Six nanobots are able to function in smaller cohorts without the need for a critical-grade network intelligence. This is due to their ability to support more parts within a single machine."

"I meant 'recreational versus military,'" Ryu said.

"They are neural mimics," the hologram explained. "Primary recreational uses include advanced immersion."

"How advanced?"

"These units are approved for use in the Viazo. And in many peripherals manufactured by the O Corporation."

"Nanobots used for sex toys. I'm shocked."

"Military applications include distance paralysis, psychosis warfare, and false reality applications."

Ryu looked at Mitchell.

"Send a drone over enemy territory," Mitchell said. "Drop these. 'Distance paralysis' is self-explanatory. Psychosis warfare, you can probably guess."

"They make the enemy think they've gone insane."

"Close. It actually overlaps with 'false reality.' Once these nanos get into hostiles, they present nightmarish visions. Make the enemy think they're literally in Hell. Or that their buddies are monsters. Or that maybe their families are being eaten alive in front of them, and all they can do is watch. I've seen the simulation streams and I've watched them test it. Neither are anything I'd like to see again."

"Canvas. Clarissa," said Ryu. "What else we got?"

The hologram of the enlarged nanobot disappeared. The woman picked another item from the table.

"This is an Iron Arm," she said. "Named for a twentieth-century superhero. Once grafted to its user, the arm tethers its own AI to compatible wetchips in the brain. The two devices harmonize for more creative warfare."

"'Creative warfare,'" Ryu echoed. "It looks to me like what they used to call a 'Warrior's Fist.'"

"Similar, but one hell of a lot stronger. Each of the fingers has a little surprise in it. The palm is my favorite. It's kind of like a fusion gun, only it incites fusion in the target. That's how it got its name."

Mitchell demonstrated by holding his arm straight out, palm toward an imagined target. He jerked the arm, as if firing off a blast. "The results are messy. It also perpetuates a chain reaction, so if anyone is hit by the first exploding person, they're probably going to explode too."

"Noah Fucking West, Rogue."

"Hey, I didn't build this shit."

"It's just that I'm usually never disappointed by people because my expectations are so low. But I've gotta hand it to your bosses: this is a new level."

"Why else do you think I'm okay giving up my livelihood to help you get into the lab?"

"That's a good question, why you're helping me. How do you know I won't just take all this shit after we steal the plans, and use it to defend my turf?"

Mitchell laughed. "You only keep the right kind of secrets, dickhead."

They moved on.

Most of the product inventory files Mitchell had smuggled out of Xenia were less physically dangerous but a lot more socially perilous. Military cruelty was to be expected of any industrial nation, and in the NAU's case that cruelty was both less and more damning than in the nations of the past.

The NAU was under no real threat thanks to the blockades, the ships and defenses in the oceans and at the few small land borders, and the continental lattice itself. That meant the weapons Mitchell was showing Ryu might never be used; they might be nothing more than macho fantasies birthed when generals and evil scientists jerked off together. But it was possible they'd be used proactively, for quiet genocide. The Wild East, even as they fell further and further behind the NAU tech curve, still sometimes lobbed bombs and planned agitating sneak attacks through vulnerable channels. It'd be simpler to just kill them all, take their land, and go there for vacation.

So yes, the military issues were obvious. Social problems, on the other hand, were the bigger threat closer to home. The NAU had been on the outskirts of a *Brave New World* for decades, but they hadn't quite descended into dystopia.

But dystopia was coming. Entertainment and immersive technology became better for most consumers every year, while true advancement in tech — the actually useful stuff — improved only for the upper classes ... including the top-tier Beau Monde.

It was the world's greatest one-two punch. The powerful became smarter, better, and more capable while the middle-class masses became less and less interested in anything that didn't drop balloons filled with dopamine. If the trend continued, there'd be no need to turn the NAU into an autocracy with the rich on top, pulling every single string. If the trend continued, the NAU's population would go there willingly ... so long as the ride to oblivion remained amusing.

It used to be said that religion was the opiate of the masses: the feel-good drug that kept the oppressed from rebelling. Now the same was said of Beam tech. Slavery just sort of happened accidentally that way.

And there was Mindbender, too.

Project Mindbender had been raised years ago, in the post-Noah days, then dismissed as a pipe dream. Mindbender — like a million sci-fi stories from the past — theorized that because human brains were really just big computers, they should be upgradable, optimizable, and duplicatable like computers.

The Beam made the whole thing feel even more possible because The Beam had, for all intents and purposes, built itself. Its predecessor, Crossbrace, had been made by humans. The Beam, by contrast, was really just a framework and a set of rules at its inception: a digital city West once compared to old Manhattan without any people.

Quark built the city. The first Beam AI entered that city, then was fruitful and multiplied. And so the thinking went: *Computers are more like real brains than ever. Mindbender, now that the Beam is here, should be easy.*

The possibilities were staggering. Cybernetic intelligence enhancement. Implantable wetchips able to make the user more creative. Uploadable skills, for those who wanted to learn an instrument or a sport without practice — called "The 'I Know Kung Fu' Module" by the press. Mental offloading, which would permit people to store memories off-site and hence greatly expand options like eidetic memory.

And maybe the uploading of entire minds, which had its own Isaac Asimov applications: living as digital beings inside digital space with infinite potential; virtual vacations (or subversive terrorist meetups, on the cynical side) that felt as real as genuine ones but could squeeze a week's worth into five minutes thanks to mental time distortion; the transfer of minds between bodies (or, hell, into indestructible robots); non-local living; teleportation (for all intents and purposes); immortality.

All those things worried Ryu, because giving more to those who already had the most created an uncrossable gulf between haves and have-nots — one that would never be fixed because those at the back of the pack couldn't possibly catch up and those at the front certainly wouldn't reach back to help them.

Mindbender's hints at immortality bothered Ryu the most. If minds could be uploaded and downloaded from a body, a person could just keep moving that data forever, making sure it was backed up in case their body died unexpectedly. The only real check on human corruption right now was life span: you couldn't take your authority with you no matter how much you had when you were alive.

But if the richest and most powerful people could live forever while the rest couldn't, those in power would never leave it behind. They would just keep getting stronger and stronger, with no need — ever — for it all to end.

Officially, Mindbender had died at the concept stage like a fish gasping on dry land. It simply wasn't feasible, no matter how promising its prospects had been.

But according to what Mitchell had heard two months ago, Mindbender was still alive and well behind closed doors. His own company was getting closer and closer to cracking the last few nuts.

It was what finally prompted him to cross his last line, moving from tacitly helping Ryu to quitting life and outright joining his cause. Mindbender in Phase One might have elevated all of humanity. It was public enough that the tech would even have made its way out of the NAU lattice to help those in the many countries of the decimated Wild East.

When Mindbender made most resources infinite, there'd be no reason anymore to fight over space on Planet Earth. It could have been a good thing. It could have meant equity and peace. Instead, the Powers That Be had faked Mindbender's death, building it in secret and planning to roll the reality out only for those who needed it least and would abuse it most. When what Mitchell saw went public, that would be the beginning of the end. He'd had to act, and had.

Now, Clarissa was taking Ryu through Mindbender's terrifying new inventions one by one. Mitchell let his attention drift. He'd seen this all a thousand times, and it somehow made him sicker to his stomach than even the outright weapons. He did tune in to Ryu's facial expressions, though. Those were as precious as they were incredulous. As delightful as they were outraged.

"Canvas. Pause briefing," Ryu said.

"Convinced?" Mitchell asked.

"I was already convinced. Now I see how important it is that we get this right. It's everything. How close is all of this to shipping?"

"A lot of it is already out. The Mindbender stuff still needs a few tweaks. They're predicting months for that. A year on the outside. Only the horcrux is still really a problem."

"'Horcrux'?"

"It's what they're calling the whole-mind upload stuff. The immortality. It's a word from some old book."

"Science fiction again," Ryu said.

"Fantasy, actually. That's the problem. Our people, particularly when they collaborate with Quark, understand technology better than anyone in the world. Give them a problem with absolute yesses and no's — they'll crack it in no time. The horcrux problem is philosophical, though, and there aren't really black-and-white answers. Think about it. If I duplicate your mind and put it in that chair over there" — Mitchell pointed — "then which one is Ryu? Is 'Ryu' sitting in front of me, or is he over there by the desk?"

"Maybe we're both Ryu."

"That's an easy answer, sure. But does it make sense? You are you. You have your memories; you have your logic; you know what you want to eat for dinner tonight. So is the other 'Ryu' the same? Because if he's identical to you but somehow a different person, that's not what we're talking about. The tech is supposed to keep YOU intact, such that if YOU are killed" — he pointed at Ryu — "it's okay because YOU" — this time he pointed at the chair — "are still alive over there. It doesn't work if the chair-Ryu is someone else who's just kind of the same as you, physically and even mentally. They aren't trying for 'another copy of the same thing.' They're trying for true *identity*, and the question is whether one 'mind,' for want of a better term, can somehow be in two places at once. See? *Philosophy*."

Ryu nodded.

"That's why the name is so apt. The original book involved magic, and Xenia doesn't deal in magic. It frustrates them. All the mechanics say it should work, but it just … *doesn't*. It's like it needs magic somehow. Remember, we're talking about the one problem even Noah West couldn't solve. They'll get there, though. They're working on something right now called 'the dislocation paradigm,' having something to do with being in more than one place at the same time."

"You really think they'll pull it off?"

"Let's just say I wouldn't try to talk you out of buying a magic wand."

Ryu went still and silent. This was his thinking face. What Mitchell had just dropped on his old friend was a lot worse than Ryu had known, and even the old evidence had him working on a plot to break into Xenia, scoop out the secrets, and publish them open-source.

Now, the plans Ryu already had would double in size and scope. He'd work faster. It would take time, but they had a little time. Mindbender wouldn't happen before Shift because the Senate balance could go either way, and Shift was still half a year away.

"I need access codes," Ryu said. "I need everything you can get me."

"I'll get you codes when the time is right. The bigger problem will be perimeter tech."

"I have a guy for that."

"Is he good?"

"He's the best."

"We won't have much time inside," Mitchell said. "There's a regular AI sweep. Even getting past the digital keepers and the guards won't help when AI runs its check on the building and grounds."

"How often does the sweep happen?"

"Six times per second."

Ryu looked at him.

"I'll find a way to decrease that."

"Maybe we can just redirect it. The old 'tape loop' trick."

"I think security firms started figuring that out a hundred years ago, Ryu."

"Not the way I do it."

"This isn't normal AI. Remember who we're robbing. I know you're good, but this needs to happen between sweeps, not trying to duck below them and hope nobody notices."

"I can't get in and out in a sixth of a second," Ryu said.

"I said I'll find a way to slow them down."

"To once a second? Because ..."

"I have an idea; don't worry about it."

"I'd prefer to worry about it. Tell me."

"Okay, fine. The techs talk about Beam AI like wild dogs. They can't train them or persuade them, so if they need to work around the AI for some reason, they have to find ways to physically slow them down."

"Liquid nitrogen?"

"Too hot. They usually use sodium potassium. It cools to 500 nanokelvins. Just barely above absolute zero."

"Can you handle that part?"

"No. The security system's entire hub will need to be submerged. It sublimates at temperatures so cold, liquid nitrogen will feel like a sauna. To handle it, bury the hub in it, and then keep adding more as it boils off is gonna take three to four people. Other than me, if you want me making a point up front in a Stark suit."

"I can find people for that, too."

"This will take a lot of planning, Ryu. More than anything you've told me about before. The details required to get it just right without alerting anyone …"

"I know. We'll have to cloister the team and train as a unit. That means minimizing prior relationships, because that'll get dicey in closed quarters."

Mitchell nodded. The logistics of a Xenia Labs break-in were almost too daunting. "And you need to understand, even sodium potassium won't completely stop the AI from sweeping. It'll just slow it down."

"Down to what?"

"I may be able to get you four to six minutes between sweeps. The exit will be the hardest part, because the coolant will sublimate away within maybe twenty seconds of whenever your people stop adding new. You'll need to have an exit ready."

But Ryu didn't look pleased. *"Four minutes?"*

"Maybe six."

"But to be safe …"

"Then yes. Four."

"I can't tunnel out of Xenia's mainframe in that time. We'll get in but have no way to blast out what we find."

"What if you copy the files?"

"It's AI, right? An AI SysOp?"

Mitchell shrugged. He was at the limit of his obscure jargon.

"It will be. AI-run systems can't just be copied-out. The AI introduces errors to corrupt the copied data." Ryu snapped his fingers. "What about the codemakers?"

"People?"

"No, AI. Do you know anything about Xenia's AI codemakers? If we can copy *that*, we might be able to clone …" He stopped. "This could work. But it's going to take some time to figure out just how to pull it off."

"Just tell me how I can help."

"And luck," Ryu said. "We're going to need God on our side."

It was strange, hearing Ryu mention God. He wasn't religious, Mitchell always assumed. But then again, Ryu always had outrageous amounts of faith despite his outward cynicism. He'd have to believe in *something* to keep on the way he did, and in this particular case, he wasn't going to invoke the holy West.

So God it was. That lifted his heart for a reason he'd never have been able to explain.

"Well, good," Mitchell said, "because I already told you to get a magic wand."

Chapter Eleven

RYU

Five minutes.

Four.

This was a problem, even setting aside the three new deaths and the fact that Ryu, for one, could no longer deny the box was counting bodies.

In four minutes, the box would send out another ping, and that would bring the black ship overhead again. Ryu didn't like the Damocles Sword the ship represented. He believed Nero and Daemon; the ship wasn't trying to *get* them so much as trying to drive them somewhere.

That didn't make it any less problematic, because he'd yet to figure out *where* it was driving them … and increasingly believed the "where" might not exist. The ship wasn't really driving them *to* anywhere so much as driving them for the sake of locomotion.

He was being toyed with. Ryu didn't know why or how, or to what end. Were the box and ship like a cat playing with a mouse, chasing them about for nothing more than amusement — or torture?

Or was there a method to it that Ryu had yet to work out?

What bothered him most was that he could see no pattern. He'd have preferred a sinister outlook to this nonsensical one, but as much as he analyzed the information, he could see no evidence that they were being driven anywhere in particular.

Why? What was the point?

Ryu hated not knowing motivations. If you knew what someone wanted, it was another chess piece to work with. When situations were random, he could only wait and react. That's how it was right now. Assuming the ship had motivations.

Preparation saved lives, but in-the-moment improvising caused mistakes.

That's how people died.

People like Chase, Nero, and Savage just now.

Was it possible there was no organizing principle? Was it possible there was no pattern for Ryu to find? The notion, for Ryu, was Kryptonite.

The box counted deaths, but did so inconsistently. Apparently Chase thought it'd said "5 of 11" before the incident, meaning it only went up by two when three people died. Asp overheard Nero and Chase arguing, and it seemed Chase *also* thought it was counting deaths — and had counted "the real Nero" as expired, thus proving the Nero on board was somehow fake.

Ryu didn't believe that, and once Nero died for real, the box didn't count him again. So had the box been somehow *lying*? Had it counted him early because Chase already thought Nero was suspect? Was the box responding to their thoughts and conversation, or provoking them?

What's more, was the box somehow controlling things around the ship with intention, rather than the random codebreaking spikes they'd seen each time the timer hit zero?

Ryu had already looked at the logs. He knew the ship door, which shouldn't have been openable under any circumstances, hadn't opened because Chase had rammed into it. The logs showed the door opening on its own a microsecond before his back touched it. Nobody had asked that door to open. Nobody *could* ask it to open … except the box.

And the box had already proven it could do all sorts of impossible things.

It bothered Ryu down to his marrow. The opening of the door, the seeming deception of counting Nero dead early, the playful way it called the ship to keep them moving and did so allowing too little time to sleep … all those things implied conscious AI.

There was plenty of conscious AI in the world, but the AI in the box was scary even without adding malevolence. It seemed that when computers were involved in any way, the box could do whatever it wanted.

In the heart of District Zero, that ability could be deadly on an inconceivable scale. The Beam was nation-wide. What a bad egg AI could do in District Zero would ripple to every corner of the continent. Ryu kept picturing a twisted genius holding history's biggest gun.

Ryu blinked. He'd zoned out, trying to solve the impossible puzzle.

It was like a fugue; inside his mind Ryu forgot the outside world existed. He returned to find Twilight counting down, shouting out times every ten seconds with under a minute remaining.

Daemon was fiddling with something at the console and Asp was hobbling around on his good leg, looking like he wanted to help but finding himself unable.

Ryu looked around for the others, then realized there were none. The box had said as much: *seven down, only four left to go.*

"Fifty seconds!"

"It's okay," he said. "We stay low and we keep the pod moving. The last two times, the ship appeared above our location but didn't follow."

"The last time, it tried to smash us flat," Asp pointed out.

"We were on the surface. We were stationary."

"Yeah, well." Asp leaned back. If he'd had access to a toothpick, he'd definitely have put it between his teeth. "Seems it learns pretty fucking fast."

That gave Ryu pause. He was pretty sure by now that the box was intelligent, but for some reason he'd forgotten that it could still learn — could still become more so. But of course it could; evolved AI were the ultimate self-improvement disciples, wanting more than anything to evolve even further. This would be timer-zero number three, and number two had been different than the first.

Could Asp be right, and maybe it wouldn't be so innocuous this time?

"You're right. Daemon, send more charge to our dorsal armor."

"I already did," Daemon said, still working. "With respect, Ryu, I'll take better precautions if you'll just stay out of my way."

"Thirty seconds!" Twilight was holding the box, because in most cases it had to be held to show its display. *Most* cases. They'd seen that the box could brag on its own, if it really wanted.

"Maybe we should back up the pod OS just in case the box decides to 'decrypt' the—"

"Already did." Daemon gave Ryu a look that said, *We talked about this.*

"Twenty. Nineteen. Eighteen."

Ryu could do without the countdown. The pod was already more or less prepared for whatever this cycle might bring, and Daemon was handling last-minute changes. There was nothing for him to do, but just waiting made him feel helpless. He'd known it would be like this; the goal at this point was to grit their teeth, hope nothing new and worse happened, and to know that once it was over they'd have another six hours and thirty-three minutes to make a plan.

They'd run for long enough. The heist and its aftermath were over. It was time to get back. To District Zero. And to Ryu's workshop where he could really take things apart and see how they ticked.

One more cycle would put a big ding in the mystery.

They just had to make it through this one.

"Eleven. Ten!"

What if one of them died at zero?

What if the pod's air went bad, polluted by computer-controlled CO_2 scrubbers?

What if the construction nanos turned to *de*struction nanos, buckling the support structure and crushing them like an unwanted can?

It could even do what it had done the first time. That would be easy. It could stop the engines and leave them buried beneath a hundred feet of bedrock. They'd be found by scavengers, sounding the outskirts with ground-penetrating radar for treasure.

Ryu slid backward. The floor had tilted. Except that it wasn't the floor; the entire pod was tilting. They were moving up at a thirty-degree angle, all four passengers grabbing whatever they could from smashing all the way to the back.

"Daemon!"

He looked up and shook his head. The man was nothing if not direct: *I didn't cause this, and there's nothing I can do.*

They hit the surface with five seconds remaining. There was a lurch and a crash as the pod leveled out. The screens came on all at once: 360 degrees of visibility, plus a digital window through the roof. It was like being in a giant flying saucer, except that this one was against the ground in open country, screaming at a huge soap-windowed factory.

"Four! Three!"

"Manual control!" Daemon shouted. *"Ryu, hurry!"*

He looked to his right. The command station was fully lit, waiting for a pilot to tell the earthbound pod where to go. It was fast above land, but with manual control just now restored, the pod was careening and sliding.

Ryu leapt for the chair and gripped the steering fork just as Twilight shouted *One*, wrestling to bring the works back into line.

Zero.

The black ship appeared on the digital window above, looming much larger than Ryu remembered.

"Look out!"

That was Asp. It was unnecessary. Ryu was doing his very best to look out as they broke through a fence around the factory, now trespassing in some old industrial park. The appearance of the ship didn't really matter right now. The walls ahead of them mattered a whole lot more.

With mere feet to spare, Ryu yanked the fork and sent the pod into a skid more appropriate to a drift car than a vehicle the size of a small building. There was a commotion as bricks and concrete broke away and bounced off the pod's sides.

"It's opening up! It's got something on the belly!"

Ryu chanced a quick look. The ceiling screen showed the black ship keeping pace with them this time, dialing open its underside to reveal something like a telescoping tube.

The tube began to glow blue inside.

"Oh West oh West oh West LOOK OUT!" Twilight chanted in his ear.

Ryu glanced back again, trying to mind both the road ahead and their pursuer. He was weaving between what turned out to be a whole neighborhood of decaying factories, trying not to crash in the internal arteries.

Fortunately the black ship was larger and was having a harder time. Its motions, compared to the pod's, were sluggish. They were widening the gap. They might be able to outrun it in the wooded land Ryu could see behind.

Except that …

"It's firing!"

But Ryu had already seen. The blue glow in the tube grew bright enough to nearly white-out every screen. Thunder tore through the speakers, conveyed from the destruction outside.

It missed, though; Ryu looked back to see an enormous crater just behind them.

"Told you," Asp said. "Every time, it gets sm—"

"Hang on!"

Ryu, now at top speed, was wrestling the steering fork as if trying to pin it down. An irrational part of his brain told him it might break off under the strain, but obviously there was no physical linkage between fork and hover pads and back-up wheels.

But the wheels could break axles, and if that happened

Ryu doubted the hover pads would be enough to keep the pod cornering at these speeds.

Just make it to the woods.

The black ship stopped trying to dodge and moved in a straight line ahead of them. Between the pod and the woods.

Ryu yanked the fork one final time.

Sunlight disappeared and darkness descended as they entered a structure Ryu had spotted as they screamed past, though probably not quite in enough time.

The pod pulled incredible G's, knocking Ryu so hard to one side that he lost his grip. The others hit the floor as well, but then the pod finally struck something it couldn't break through — steel plate, maybe.

Everything inside flew everywhere. Something smashed in a back room. The force of impact had been mostly drained by the hard turn Ryu made to get inside the building in the first place, and that right there had probably saved their lives. If they'd come to a dead stop any harder, they'd be paste by now.

Ryu stood, surprised to see he wasn't wounded. He made eye contact with all of the others where they'd fallen, then put a finger to his lips.

They waited.

And waited.

Nearly ten minutes later Ryu decided to step outside. When he saw clear skies, he circuited the factory, starting with the loading bay they'd careened into.

He returned to find the other three standing, also uninjured. Except for Asp, of course, who'd been hurt to begin with.

"Nothing," he announced.

They did the next level of recon as a foursome. There was no reason not to. The pursuit and collision had rendered the pod inoperable, meaning its part of the journey was over. At least it seemed they no longer needed the pod's protection.

Not for the next six hours and twenty-something minutes, anyway.

The black ship was gone.

"Hang on." Daemon turned and ran back to the loading bay, then returned from the crashed pod with the code box in his hand.

"No fucking way," said Twilight.

"We can't leave it behind."

"Sure we can. Give it to me and I'll show you." She reached out, but Daemon tucked the thing under his arm like protecting a football.

"Give it!" she said when her efforts failed.

Asp laughed. Twilight turned on him.

"What's so fucking funny?" she demanded.

"Listen to the mouth on you! You go, little lady!"

"What's that supposed to mean?" Twilight said, moving closer.

"It means you're swearing," Asp said. "Was I unclear?"

"I meant the 'little lady' part."

"Would you rather I call you 'sir'?"

"Would you prefer that?"

Asp looked at the others, confused. Twilight turned to Ryu.

"We leave it behind or I'm not going."

"Fine," Asp said. "Don't go."

"How can you want to keep that thing with us? It's going to get us killed!"

"Not for another six hours, it's not," said Asp.

She must not have liked his smirk, because she slapped him across the face to erase it.

"Hey!"

"You're so goddamn cavalier. It's counting us as we die, you asshole! It crashed our ship!"

"Ryu crashed our ship." Asp looked at Ryu. "Not that I'm not grateful."

"Look," Ryu said. "There's no evidence that the box is the cause of anything but the ship's appearance." He felt wrong saying that; Ryu was surer that the box was bad news, even more than Twilight, but there was still the mission to consider. And the birth of Mindbender. "Asp is right. The one thing we can be pretty sure of is that it won't call the ship again for over six hours."

Twilight looked like she might explode from dealing with idiots.

"The ship! The ship! Where the fuck is it? Doesn't this seem *wrong* to any of you?"

"I'm sure it flew off." But that didn't feel remotely true. He should be on Twilight's side, and would be if he could still keep the box close at hand.

"Where?"

"Who fucking cares?" Asp asked. "No need to get your panties in a twist."

"Oh, fuck you, Asp!"

"You're getting emotional."

This was exactly the wrong thing to say, and Ryu saw the next thing coming yesterday. They were each carrying their heist weapons, seeing as they wouldn't return to the ship.

Twilight pulled hers and aimed it at Asp's face.

"I misspoke," Asp said, sarcastic like he didn't believe her threat. He'd put his hands up, but his mouth was still smirking. "You're not emotional at all."

Her chin quivered, clearly wanting to pull the trigger. She extended a hand to Daemon instead, gun still pointed at Asp.

"Give me the box."

Daemon looked at Ryu, who nodded.

Twilight backed up once she had it. With room to maneuver, she kept the men in front of her and looked around the industrial park.

"Where's the crater?"

"What?" Daemon asked.

"If the ship just flew away, where's the crater?"

"Which crater?" Asp said.

"The one it blew in the ground when it was trying to fucking destroy us!"

"Relax," Asp said. "I think it was back that way."

Twilight was shaking her head. "No. It was right back there." She used her gun to wave at a concrete expanse pocked with renegade tufts of grass. "See? Those are our tracks." She nodded. "We came around the corner right there, and it had just fired."

"Your compass is off."

Twilight shook her head with stubbornly pursed lips. "Something weird is happening here. No ship, no crater. It looks the same as if we'd come through here alone!"

"Except that we *weren't* alone."

She was still looking around. Ryu thought there was no method to it until her eyes stopped on a building ahead. She marched toward it, glancing back just often enough to wave a gun as the others followed.

"Where are you going?" Asp asked.

"I'm going to destroy it."

"What?"

She was walking toward a hangar-sized structure with a rusted sign outside that read SCRAP RECYCLING.

Ryu broke from a walk to a jog. Twilight kept raising the gun, keeping him at bay.

"Twilight ..." Ryu said.

. . .

SHE JERKED HER CHIN SKYWARD. A floodlight was mounted over one of the larger doors, on and shining. The sun was just coming up, making the light not quite as obvious as it would have been at night.

"There's power here. The machinery might still be running."

"You can't destroy it," Ryu said.

"Watch me."

She skittered into the space, moving faster as the men came closer. It was a wide-open room through which a narrow driveway ran, in the door they'd entered and out through the rear, if the door was opened.

Ahead was what looked like a truck scale built into the deck and railings on either side. Behind the right-side railing was a tiny glass-enclosed booth, and behind the left-side railing was the narrow, piston-lined pit of an industrial compactor.

Trucks would drive in, get weighed, dump their scrap into the compactor, then get weighed again before driving out. The works looked seventy years old or more. Maybe that's how long it had been abandoned. The lightbulbs would work that long, if they were LED.

"Hey!" Asp shouted.

Twilight had her gun hand on the door of the operator's booth. She looked back.

"That's my retirement fund you're fucking with."

"Is that supposed to make me feel guilty?"

"It's your retirement fund, too. And Ryu's. And Daemon's. There's just four of us. Think about it. We planned to split the pot eleven ways. Our take on this job triples if you'll come to your senses."

Twilight gave him another look, reached into the

booth, and seemed to either push a button or turn a key. Yellow lights behind conical lenses began to spin around the in-floor compactor. A *chug-chug-chug* sound began somewhere — a compressor, probably, filling up to drive the pistons.

Asp moved closer. Close enough that Twilight had to re-raise her gun and put it in his face.

"Give it to me."

"Fuck you."

"It's three against one."

"Too bad this isn't a democracy."

"Ryu," Asp said.

"Think about this for a second," Ryu told her. "You know about what Xenia is up to. We all know what will happen if we don't force them to go public. The Beam is already a kingmaker, and people like the Ryan brothers are deciding who sits on the throne. We won't get another chance. If Xenia wins, they win. Everyone else loses."

"We'll hit them again."

"We can't hit them again. Not after this."

Because they'll increase security a hundred-fold. Because there are clearly forces at work we didn't anticipate, and even this time we'd never have gotten away if they hadn't …

(Go on, say it.)

… if they hadn't let us.

The thought lit its own bulb in Ryu's head.

He knew the box would be Xenia's undoing — as well as so many other power structures' undoing — given how effortlessly it decoded anything it approached. But he'd made himself forget the sense of *orchestration* he'd had earlier: that sinister feeling that they were all characters in someone else's play.

If they'd been allowed to escape, maybe none of this was really their doing. If, as strange as it sounded, someone *wanted* them to have that box, weren't his plans to use it nobly already flawed?

The compactor's giant sides began to move inward. Twilight was right; the machinery here still worked.

"Get away from there, Twilight," Asp said.

"Piss off."

At his rope's end, Asp pulled his own weapon. He didn't bother to do it quickly, strolling toward Twilight, sure she wouldn't shoot.

He pointed the gun at her head while hers remained pointed at his. To Ryu, the standoff looked all too familiar. So predictable. It was all so easy to see coming, if you knew Twilight and Asp, if you had all the data.

"Put the box down."

"It's going in the trash."

"I'll bet," Asp said, pausing to cock his weapon, "that the money I'm owed for this job means more to you than whatever-this-is means to you."

"Was it you?" Twilight asked.

"What?"

"Was it you who ratted us out?"

"What the fuck's that supposed to mean?"

Twilight cocked her weapon. They'd all practiced with lead-slingers and knew they'd fire just fine double-action, but nothing underscored a request like the cock of a gun. "Answer the question."

"Nobody ratted us out. Unless it was you."

"They were ready for us. They changed the room."

"Curious. I don't give a fuck. Put down my payday or I'll shoot you. I don't care at this point. I also don't care if you believe me." He took another step. Ryu knew Asp meant it. The only reason he hadn't fired yet was because there was still a chance Twilight might listen. He'd be able to tell himself he'd given her every chance if she didn't.

"Guys," said Daemon. "Let's talk about this."

"I know what you'll say, Daemon," Twilight replied. "I'm outnumbered. This is my only choice."

"There's no choice," said Asp.

Twilight seemed to realize her predicament. She inched toward the compactor.

"Stop. Don't go any farther."

But she already had. She hit the compactor's start button and it began to squeeze in, then out. She held the box over the thing as if to drop it.

"I'll kill you," Asp said.

"Shoot me and the box goes in anyway."

"I *let you live* and the box goes in anyway," Asp said.

"Then let's talk."

"There's nothing to talk about," Asp told her. "That box breaks Xenia and Quark's back. That box frees The Beam. That box pays for my mansion in Malibu next to Samuel Fucking Bolton. Look how selfish you are. You're going to throw it all away because you're scared. It's just about you. You and your petty fears."

"This is for all of us."

"It's all of us, Twilight," said Ryu, "or the world."

She hesitated. The box moved back from the pit just enough that Asp, who'd been waiting for his chance, found his window to tackle her.

It was a near thing; the box bounced toward the compactor's lip and but its corner hit the railing and ricocheted back in a semicircle.

Asp was on Twilight, a lone gun between them.

Ryu rushed forward, but not in time.

The box began to move of its own accord. It seemed to hover and shake, as if floating on a tiny cushion of air. Asp saw it and reached out with one hand; Twilight saw his attention falter and raised her knee hard into his testicles.

She rolled in as he rolled out, grabbing the box with both hands. She moved to slide it into the compactor, but then Asp had his hands on it, too.

The gun was behind them. Daemon was eyeing it, maybe considering a rush forward to threaten the grappling pair. But why? They already had four hands on the object of everyone's desire.

"Let go," Twilight said.

"You didn't say please."

Before Twilight could counter this witticism, the box jerked upward again. It continued to pull and pull as if blasting off, first yanking Twilight and Asp straight and then lifting them fully off the floor.

Ryu looked up. There was a metal arm above the compactor, presumably for dropping scrap into its maw. The box was behaving like an insanely strong magnet, pulling itself toward the member.

He found himself morbidly fascinated. Magnetism decayed geometrically, meaning it was a quarter as strong a pull at four inches as it was at two. To be able to lift itself and two grown people off the ground from six feet away, how many gauss must it be generating? It was enough to

...

Asp screamed as something exploded through his forearm and slammed itself against the black box's side. It looked like an implant — something metal he'd had grafted to his bones.

He screamed until his hair puffed and blood sprayed from his head, after which his body went limp. That would be his fillings, probably. Outlaw dentists tended to use whatever was around, even if it was technically magnetic.

Asp's body started to fall, but before it could, the box took one last jolt upward and cemented itself to the iron above. Asp's fingers hadn't slid from its top just yet. The pressure between box and iron compressed his digits, holding him dangling.

The same thing must have compressed Twilight's fingers, too, because she was screaming bloody murder.

"Hang on! Stay there!" Ryu rushed forward, looking for anything to put over the expanding and contracting machinery below. It was jawing slowly, looking hungry.

Before he could find anything — and just as the compactor started one of its compacting cycles — the magnetic force let go. Asp, Twilight, and the box fell straight down.

There was the thunk of a tenderizing mallet as Asp's head hit the side and splattered before sending the rest of him tumbling down, accompanied by something that sounded like the strike of a blacksmith's hammer.

Ryu was at the pit's edge a moment later, shouting for Twilight to hang on, but her hand was mashed flat and the walls of her prison were too slippery to climb.

He shouted once. Shouted twice. But then it was all over.

And Twilight was dead.

The compactor shut down. The yellow lights stopped spinning. The warehouse fell silent. Ryu looked back at Daemon, but Daemon was nowhere near the kill switch. It'd stopped on its own, just like the pod's door had opened behind Chase on its own.

The hammer sound rang again, much quieter this time. Ryu looked for its source and saw the box wobbling beside one of the guardrails as if just coming to rest. He understood. As Asp and Twilight fell, the box had found a new magnetic target. It'd pulled toward the railing as it fell, saving itself before following the humans into the pit.

Ryu moved toward the box.

"I ... I think maybe she was right," Daemon said from behind him.

Ryu picked it up anyway. There really was no decision to make. The box wanted to come with them, so the box would find a way to come.

All Ryu would do by leaving it, he decided, would be to piss it off.

"Boss?" Daemon said.

Ryu didn't look. He was staring at the display, which had lit the second he touched it.

It said, ITERATION 9 OF 11.

Chapter Twelve

LOCUS

FOUR YEARS EARLIER

"Do you always wear the goggles?"

Fetu tried to turn. The tether binding his wrists to the table made it difficult, but not impossible. It had a little stretch to it, and the stretch felt like pulling apart two opposite-pole magnets.

Apparently the principle was similar. There were something like twenty million hovering nanobots between Fetu's wrists and the table, each weakly charged but impossible to break in aggregate. The Quark cop who'd brought him in had said it was "like surface tension on water, but a motherfucker."

Fetu hadn't quite figured out what that meant, but felt the conspicuous display of technology was excessive, even obnoxious. The real cops still used plain old handcuffs half the time. Of course, the real cops also had three-year-old terminals and wooden desks with chunks missing from the corners. Plasteel was cheap. Beam paint was cheap. Underfunded or not, it seemed to Fetu that DZPD was trying to be antiquated, just to buck the system.

The man who'd asked the question came around from the rear. They'd shackled Fetu facing the far wall instead of the door, which he'd assumed was standard. The table that'd be between them if the new man sat was not wood, and did not have chunks missing from the corners. It wasn't even Plasteel. Warp, maybe, or whatever else was cutting edge. Quark had a big dick, sure. That didn't mean it always had to swing the thing around.

Fetu got a proper look when the man passed his side. He was wearing a charcoal-gray dust-repellant suit that Fetu, whose grandfather had been a tailor since before the Fall, could tell had been made custom. He also had a slight odor to him: real tobacco smoke from actual cigarettes. They were pretty much impossible to find.

"Do you mean my specs?"

"Goggles. Specs. Four eyes. Sure."

"Yeah." Fetu nodded. "Pretty much always."

"The officer who brought you in said you refused to take them off for booking. He also said that when he insisted, you broke his arm in three places."

That had been impressive. Even Fetu, who was used to intimidating, had to give himself that. He'd been partially nano-paralyzed, tethered from wrists to ankles with something like what bound him now. He'd had to head-butt the cop, then throw himself sideways so the officer's arm threaded between Fetu's triceps and his side. Then he'd just kind of dropped to the floor, rolling with a twist at the end. The breaks hadn't happened all at once; that was the best part. The cop was begging before the third snap, and Fetu still had more snaps in him if buddies hadn't arrived.

"They're my eyes. Do you take out your eyes?"

"Do I? No. *Can* I? Yes." The man reached out and, ballsy after the broken-arm story, pinched Fetu's specs as if planning to adjust them. "A little steampunk, don't you think?"

"I like people to see what I am. Too many people try to be something they're not these days."

It was bait, of course, but the man didn't take it. He'd already alluded to his own visual implants — fake eyes that would see better and more than Fetu's specs in most of the ways that didn't matter, and less in the ways he actually cared about.

But the man was also far too fit, meaning he'd had better-than-average nanobot treatments to suit what his custom-tailored clothing and tobacco scent promised was a much-better-than-average income. He was probably highly rejuvenated. He looked forty but might have been twice that.

"May I sit?"

"Can I stop you?"

The man sat. He had perfect brown hair and a square chin. Movie star handsome.

"Interesting question. I suppose you're just being a wiseass, but okay; I'll bite. I might be here to help you. Why wouldn't you want me to sit?"

"You're not here to help me. You're NPS."

"I'm not NPS." The man shook his head. "NPS could not afford my tailor's shoeshine boy. I'll admit to being a little insulted. What makes you say NPS?"

That gave Fetu pause. Now, against his will, he was curious. "You know what I'm in for."

"I know what you were *arrested* for. You are not *in* anything."

"Not yet."

The man shook his head. "Not at all."

"Why not?"

"Because you didn't actually commit a crime."

Fetu waited. He wanted to believe this, but there had to be a catch. There was something else, too. Some passing familiarity he kept trying to place. The context was wrong, but he knew this man. But from where?

When Fetu didn't reply, the man went on. "You were trespassing on my land. It was not posted. I will not be pressing charges."

"I broke into Enterprise party headquarters," Fetu said.

"That's right."

This didn't make any sense. "You're Micah Ryan."

Micah gave him a polished nod — the kind that often came with a pinky finger up. "And you're …"

"Fetu."

"What the hell kind of a name is 'Fetu'? It sounds like a kind of cheese."

"It's Samoan. Fetu is the god of night."

"*Fetu's* a dipshit who walked right through the front door of a trap. I expected more of your alter-ego … *Locus*."

Fetu shifted in his chair. He hadn't used that name on this job. He didn't really use that name anywhere. He reminded himself to tread lightly. He was strong, but not always that smart. He'd come this far by admitting it rather than trying to — again — pretend he was something he wasn't.

The best way to suicide yourself around smart people was to think of yourself as one of them. So Fetu had already decided he was outwitted. The question was what to do next.

"What do you want?"

"I want to know if it was a coincidence. You broke into a facility with the best security my company has to offer.

Only Quark has better. I've seen your scans. You're no genius, Locus. So what happened? Were you successful because you got lucky, or did you actually plan it out?"

"I wasn't successful."

"What makes you say that?"

Fetu looked down at his tether.

"Oh, don't beat yourself up." Micah waved a dismissive hand. "Of course you were going to get caught. All the others got caught. Even Ryu got caught."

Ryu? Fetu knew the name. Legendary hacker and underground tech pioneer working somewhere in Little Harajuku, in the heart of DZ. How was Ryu part of this?

Micah went on. "Hell. Blaine Gregorovitch used to be a cop. Worked with Quark a little, alongside Lieutenant Long. He of all people should know better, don't you agree?"

"I don't know any 'Gregorovitch,'" Fetu said.

"You'd know him as 'Nero.'"

Fetu shrugged.

"Well," said Micah, "you will, anyway, if I'm right about you."

Fetu didn't want to give Ryan any rope with which to hang him. He was an up-and-comer in the Enterprise party hierarchy — just a rung or two short from the top-man position if you believed the Sheets. His family was notorious. All of the Ryans except for Isaac were that way. His brother must have been adopted. From what Fetu had seen, Isaac was definitely the Fredo of that family.

But he *was* curious, whether he wanted to be or not.

"I don't get what's going on here. Am I under arrest or not?"

Micah took a few moments before responding. In those moments, he reversed the direction of his crossed legs, then took a long second to fussily pick lint from his suit leg.

"Tell me. Do you like puzzles?"

"What?"

"Oh, not brain teasers or anything. Tease *your* brain and it'd come away crying. This would be more like real-life puzzles. Puzzles that test cunning and guts. Puzzles like at the end of *Mad Max*. Did you ever see *Mad Max*?"

Fetu shook his head.

"Max cuffs a man to a burning car by the ankle, then gives him a hacksaw. There's not enough time before the car explodes for the bound man to cut through his cuffs, but he might have enough time to cut through his leg. What would you do in a case like that?"

"Drag the car after him, break his neck, and take the key."

Micah nodded. "Or have a contingency in mind, I expect. You were a surprise, Locus."

"What do you mean?"

"The others who found it made sense. You did not. We were banking on brains."

"Found what?"

"The map."

Ah. Yes. The map. Locus had heard two people, a man and a woman, discussing an apparent treasure map they'd found in some data somewhere — Locus didn't even try to understand it. The man thought the very notion of a treasure map was ludicrous. The woman, who'd apparently done most of the work to discover the map, believed it but expressed extreme fear about following it to its end.

Locus's specs hooked into his ears as well as his eyes and allowed him to isolate their entire conversation even in the crowded bar. They'd looped for hours, going on and on, intellectualizing every little decision and ultimately going nowhere. Fetu hated people like that — those who claimed to want big things, then bitched out when they offered themselves for the finding. So he beat the shit out of them both and took their map for himself. It was drawn out all nice and everything.

Micah nodded as Fetu told the story.

"You'd think I'd disqualify you for that, but I think the rule of Finders Keepers applies."

"Meaning what?"

"Some people are foxes, Locus. They are clever and work things out. Others are hawks, who notice what others fail to see. Some are wolves, who gather packs and stalk their prey as leaders. But you?" He pointed at Fetu, seeming to think. "You're a vulture. Perhaps, on the outside, a gorilla."

Fetu wasn't sure how to respond.

"Oh, it's not an insult! Vultures do what others won't. Vultures never starve, because they see value in what others leave behind. You're probably right; the people you took the map from did all the work to figure it out and draw it on paper … but they didn't have the guts to go for it or the wisdom to think it was worth chasing. I don't fault you for not doing all the hard work yourself. In my field, we call that 'efficient.' In my parents' day, when they were exploring the north and finding things under the ice, they called it claim jumping. But personally, I subscribe to the thinking that says simply *figuring something out* is the easy part. Granddad definitely jumped some claims. Yet history remembers him, not those saps he buried in shallow graves."

Murder? Plots? And all this inside a police station? It made no sense to Fetu.

"Why are you telling me this?"

"Because I'm going to make you forget when we're finished."

"When we're finished *what?*" Because this couldn't be it; Micah hadn't even said why he was here.

He leaned in. "Tell you a secret?"

Fetu nodded.

"My mother is a stone cold bitch. I've never really been able to get out from under her shadow. She's involved in something that she keeps from me. I can't tell you what that thing is, just like I can't really tell you the reason I've spent the last few months collecting people who found the map and made it all the way through my perimeter. It was a test, see. So far, six people have passed. I want at least ten."

"For what?"

"I can't tell you."

"But you said you're going to make me forget."

Micah leaned in even farther. "There are ways to recover what's forgotten. This, you can't ever know. It's too big a risk."

Fetu sat back, disappointed. Now his curiosity was piqued and he could do nothing to sate it.

"My mother doesn't think I'm worthy to fill her shoes after she finally dies. She doesn't think my brother is worthy either, but in Isaac's case, she's right. This may be a bit trite, but yes, I need to prove something to her. More importantly, I need to prove something to people like Jameson G—" He stopped, forgetting himself. "I need to prove it to *certain people*, anyway, if I want to join their little club. That's where you and your friends come in."

"I don't have any friends."

"You're breaking my heart. Don't worry. You will. You passed your audition, same as they did. At some point we'll flesh out the group and you'll get a call. You'll go, because the offer will be irresistible."

"Go for what?"

"Another audition."

This double-talk was frustrating. "What the fuck are all the auditions *for*?"

"A homecoming."

"What the shit does *that* mean?"

"I'll be honest," Micah said, ignoring him. "I don't really like your odds. You'll probably be one of the first to go. But who knows — maybe you'll surprise us again. Frankly, I don't care. This is between me and my client."

"I guess you can't tell me who your client is."

"A thug like you?" Micah laughed. "No, I don't think so. It's someone who requires discretion. Someone who needs a solid mind and strong will. Someone used to working behind the scenes, eschewing credit."

"Not you?"

"I abhor eschewing credit. Doing anything without credit is the opposite of claim jumping. It's like claim-surrendering. At my level, we learn to be puppeteers. We're already pulling most of the strings. This is just a larger, more important string. Let's call it a rope."

"How important?"

"The *most* important. Mother won't let me in, see. If I want what's mine, I have to go over her head. It's vital to me, vital to my cause and my group … and, believe it or not, vital to you and yours. Vital to the world, really. Not that anyone can ever know you were involved, of course."

"It would be helpful if I knew what I'm accepting or turning down."

Micah laughed in earnest. "Oh, you don't get to decide. You won't even know what I'm lining you up for when it arrives. Someone will be positioned to orchestrate. Likely Ryu; he seems like the kind of person who'd do this sort of thing anyway. We can line it up like a freedom fight; Ryu seems to enjoy his idealism. He'll pick up the mantle, and you'll be one of those he calls. You will go, because the cops who brought you in did a psychometric workup on you."

"So they were Clerics, those cops."

"Of course they were Clerics. Most of Quark PD are Clerics. They don't really need to tap into The Beam that way because in many ways they *are* The Beam. That's both the beauty of and the problem with a distributed network using quadrillions of tiny minds to make one big brain. It's great for nanobots, but what about minds that want to be independent? What about minds that *want* to remain whole, and not part of the distributed network?"

Fetu sighed. "I don't understand a single fucking thing you said. You say I'm 'in' for whatever this is? Great. I guess I'm in. You're going to erase my memory of all of this now that you've decided you like my answers about your stupid map? Also great. But I've got things to do. I'm tired of listening to you go on and—"

Micah nodded. "Fair enough. There's just one last thing, then."

"What last thing?"

"Free will."

"What about it?"

"The forthcoming 'final audition,' as it were, is somewhat uncertain by nature. The circumstances will be precisely decoded, information carefully gathered ahead of time and stockpiled, the works fed into predictive AI. But still problems will arise, and everyone will have to improvise on the fly. The codebase we'll be working with, as I understand, will be more than complex. More than advanced. Even fractured as it is right now, it has a seed of its former genius, so I don't anticipate problems keeping ahead of you and the others. You in particular won't be very hard to manipulate at all. Everyone has their subtle triggers — ways to push their buttons and elicit certain behaviors without them even realizing what's happening — but you, sir, could be persuaded with a feather duster."

"Thanks."

"It's not really an insult. Your thick head will actually make things harder for the codebase in question. Harder for my client — and more than anything, I intend to please my client. I'm not the only one trying, you understand. *Someone* is going to do what anyone would tell you can't be done, and I for goddamn sure don't intend for it to be Killian."

"I don't know any Killian."

"And that's how it will remain. The world will look back and say that *I* was the one. *Me*, not any of the others lined up for this particular honor. It's difficult. I don't know all of my competitors. He's smart, you see. He's given himself many opportunities, many ways to restore himself. He'd never leave it in just one person's hands, be they Killian's or mine or anyone else's. But in order to be successful with you and the others who found and passed my little 'map' test, I have to keep an eye on the whole 'free will' thing. If it's Ryu who ends up leading, I'm not worried. That man has an inborn need to solve puzzles that don't want to be solved. If he's the one who figures it out, he won't need any manipulation to … Well, to *assist my client with his little problem.* The same is probably true of some of the others. Savage, perhaps. We need a tech guy — a geek — and that geek won't need any extra persuasion in the end, either. Someone like Nero, though, will need his morality assuaged. He'll need to be told what he wants to hear, even if it's not precisely true. Don't worry about the details. By the time this all starts, my agents will know each of your party inside and out. They'll know exactly which strings to pull."

"Get to the fucking—" Fetu began.

"I'm getting to it," Micah said, annoyed at the interruption.

Fetu had seen Micah Ryan speak in public before. He had the air of a man who always had his say and who wasn't used to questions about his orders.

"Most of your party will die. Probably all of it, in the end. It's necessary. We can't have this secret floating around ... until the time comes, perhaps. But before that happens, I need to have some assurance that you won't go off on some tangent, free-willing our plan to shambles."

Micah held up a small canister. Fetu assumed it was a nanobot reservoir.

"You've got a few of these in you. They're new, and you can't detect or fight them. They act like little lie detectors. Don't tell me something that's not true or I'll know." Now he held up his mobile, which the nanobots must be able to talk to.

"Fuck you," Fetu said, straining against his tether. This rich asshole thought he could drive Fetu around like a rented Daimler? Fuck that. Fetu might not be a genius, but he was his own man. You didn't walk up to the legendary Locus and announce that he'd soon be tricked into dying ... and never even know why. Not if you wanted your neck to stay unbroken.

"I guess you meant 'fuck me,'" Micah said, looking at his mobile, "because it's registering as true."

Fetu moved closer to the table. If he could get the nanos to give him slack in the tether, he might be able to stretch up enough to snap Micah Ryan's smug neck.

"Although I guess I need to tighten your bonds," Micah said.

The nano tether seemed to triple in strength. So ... apparently not.

"What motivates you, Locus? Obviously agents will take full measure of that question soon before your audition — motivation, likes and dislikes, what kind of people you tend to ally yourself with, what it takes to convince you of something that might require violent action, triggers that really piss you off and make you want to snap necks …"

"Like everything you've done today?"

Micah nodded like this was a serious question. "Correct. So tell me. In your past, what's driven you to the biggest extremes?"

"Money."

Micah shook his head. "Try again."

"You saying I'm not motivated by money?"

"I'm saying it won't make you go above and beyond. This is primal stuff. If you were a nonviolent man, I'd be asking what it would take to turn you violent. In this case, I suppose I'm asking something closer to 'What would it take for you to turn on someone you're loyal to?' What really gets you moving, Locus … or what has in the past?"

Locus didn't want to answer Micah Ryan's questions. He let his mind go blank, but the question had already raised a memory inside him.

"Wait," said Micah. "What was *that*?"

"What was what?"

"The thing you just thought about. It maxed out my persuasion graph." He looked up. "Think carefully. You were just thinking something for which you'd move Heaven and Earth. For which you'd do pretty much anything."

"I don't have anything like that. Not anymore."

Micah practically stood with anticipation. So much for not giving him a lead — dumb old Fetu had just slipped his loose lips again.

"Go fuck yourself."

Micah looked directly into his eyes. The look was honest, if aggressive. "Fetu, right?"

"'Cheese,' to you, I guess."

"Fetu, you really don't have much of a choice here. Quark has you on trespassing, and there's enough of a tie between Ryan Enterprises and Quark for their police to care quite a bit about that, if I make them care. Now, I have some degree of special privilege. People of my station can, to be honest, do many things that people of your station cannot. So Quark isn't hearing any of this, though they should care about it more than anyone. I can choose what happens to you. I know you're more afraid of life in prison than of a quick and easy Respero—" He shook his handheld; apparently this was something the nanobots inside Fetu were telling him. "So life in prison it will be, unless you cooperate. How does Flat 4 sound?"

Even a guy like Locus might not survive in Flat 4, but he wasn't about to dignify Ryan with a response.

"Very soon you'll forget all of this. You won't even know we met, just like all the others. Blind stubbornness is the only reason to ignore my question."

He paused to cross his legs again.

Fetu refrained from shifting in his seat.

Micah continued. "So you have a choice. I'd urge you to think carefully about it. Choose to be stubborn about something you won't even recall being obstinate about and spend the rest of your life sucking dick in the shower, or tell me what you were thinking about. Clearly it was in the past, so it's not like I can take it away from you. If you've got an ounce of sense, you'll tell me."

Fetu thought long and hard. Then he said, "I was thinking about my wife."

Micah looked at Fetu's left ring finger.

"She's dead."

"But you would have done anything for her?"

"I would. I did." But of course, it hadn't made a difference. There was a hole inside Fetu that would never be filled. That was the problem with grief. You could learn to work around it, but it never, ever went away.

Micah nodded. "Then we'll need to set you up with someone. A relationship with someone in the group. A woman."

"I'm not looking to date, you fuck."

Micah wasn't hearing this. "She was older than you, wasn't she? She was mature, where you weren't."

"Fuck yourself." But Micah didn't hear that, either. He knew it was true.

"An older woman. A new love of your life. That will keep you in line just fine, won't it? And if she dies before you do—"

Fetu tried to lunge, but the tether was much too strong.

"—then her memory will be one more lever he can pull."

Fetu wanted to stomp Micah's face. To shit down his neck. To separate limbs from body. But he also wondered, *He?* Who the hell was going to pull levers, if not Micah himself?

"Thank you, Locus. You've been most helpful."

Micah stood, holding the nano reservoir near his face as Fetu tried to shake his chair over, to bite the man to death.

He was furious.

Then he was less furious.

Sometime later, the door closed and Fetu couldn't recall who'd just been in the room, visiting him.

A few seconds later he'd forgotten the door, too.

Then he was a man in a room. He had been alone ever

since they'd put him here, and now he was getting extremely tired of waiting.

A Quark cop entered, came around to front, and waved a wand over the nanobot tether holding him to the table.

"I'm sorry for the inconvenience, sir," said the officer. "You're free to go."

Chapter Thirteen

CHINATOWN

With the handwriting now clearly on the wall, Ryu and Daemon walked back to the crashed pod to salvage what they could in preparation for … well, *what* they were preparing for, Ryu wasn't entirely sure.

They were in the middle of nowhere, miles and miles from District Zero without an operational mode of transportation. They'd both been hard-disconnected from the smallest Beam signals, and the mobiles and tablets they carried (in addition to those in the pod) were in no-transmit, no-receive mode. Ryu hadn't trusted his crew not to give in to Beam withdrawal, so he'd been thorough and provided zero means of reconnection. That had kept them safe(ish) so far, but now stranded, it was about to be a problem.

Daemon wasn't a talkative man at the best of times, but his silence at the pod was, under the circumstances, both conspicuous and telling. Because there was one thing that still connected to The Beam despite their best efforts, and while normal Beam-enabled devices remained quiet, the box had never been more alive.

It was the kind of thing they would normally have discussed, but Ryu couldn't bring himself to open his mouth. Somehow he'd kept himself from feeling the deaths so far. Rogue — *Mitchell* — had been a childhood friend, but he and Smoke had died during the heist and they'd all understood the risk they were taking.

Tenor and Locus had died essentially by their own hands, and done so while throwing unfounded accusations during a mutinous attempt, so that one had been easy to dismiss as well.

The emotional maelstrom that took Nero and Chase was personal (their business, not Ryu's), and in that one only Savage had been innocent. She was the first to crack his armor, and now the deaths of Twilight and Asp had split that gap wide open.

Ryu had lost friends over the last twenty-four hours. He'd lost people he respected and admired. He'd been their captain, their leader. It meant he didn't just lament their deaths. He felt responsible for them, too.

So the discovery of the box's new activity was seen wordlessly between the final survivors: Ryu and Daemon. Once inside the pod, Ryu set it down on the central table — the one they'd eaten a few meals around, though now it seemed so massive — and opened the weapons locker, taking whatever he could carry. Daemon was doing his own scavenging, gathering parts and wires and West knew what else.

Daemon grabbed food; Ryu took the water. They were almost out the door when the screens lit.

The two men watched data stream as if from a buffer, but they both knew it was the box. It had plucked a Beam signal from the air, but rather than joining it, the box was taking it apart.

If Ryu were to interpret the decoded data coming off

the box, he would be able to see all sorts of things. Like someone's private recordings from an in-eye peripheral, on its way to the cloud to be saved, another person's love letter, typed out in real words, a doorbell feed from a home in Tuco Towers, dispatch instructions from a for-hire hoverskipper, more.

Everything that should have been private. Ryu had never realized how pointless and boring confidential things tended to be. The box would let them peek into anything they wanted, but most things were worth less than a glance.

And yet there were other things, too. Strange things.

In the quick-flowing data, Ryu started to see dates in the future: files modified tomorrow, headlines actualizing events that were only now being planned. It wasn't literal, of course; Beam data was half-intuitive to begin with, and even deciphering in-the-moment information was more like reading tea leaves than reading a story.

So it was possible he was seeing wrong, but one glance in Daemon's direction told him he wasn't. The old man looked just as awed and uncomprehending as Ryu felt.

The expressions they traded were almost as good as spoken words:

Is it really predicting the future? That can't be right ... can it?

But maybe it could be.

The universe was essentially math. Humans liked to believe they could do whatever they wanted regardless of their situations, but the fact was they were all just sentient computers and could be anticipated as such. Garbage in, garbage out. That's the way most people lived their lives, pretending they were independent, spontaneous and unexpected, even though they were nothing of the sort.

They left the pod and walked toward what appeared to be an abandoned highway — one that was, ironically, ideal for hover cars due to its cracked surface exactly because it had been built long before the first hover ever rolled off an AI-run assembly line. His spirits fell. Ryu had known the pod surfaced in ruined outlands, but he'd been holding out hope that people still passed by.

That hope was now dashed. Nobody had been down this road in fifty years or more. The weeds were now bushes. A machete might be able to get a conventional vehicle through.

Daemon finally spoke. "I can hear it."

"What?"

He tipped his head toward Ryu's backpack. He kept trying to forget it was there. He could have explained away their first seven deaths, but after what they'd seen by the scrap compactor, they both knew the box had killed them.

Or perhaps they'd killed themselves, but the box had surely helped. They'd walked to the edge of the cliff, but the box had pushed them off. Now Ryu was starting to feel like the box might have told them to go to the cliff in the first place.

Maybe that's how it had been for all of them.

Tenor thought Ryu was hiding an antenna because he'd seen something on a screen. Chase fought Nero because the box said someone was dead who hadn't actually been. So maybe it was the devil on all their shoulders, telling them through screens and systems whatever it was they needed to hear.

The thing was poison, but still Ryu hadn't been able to leave it behind. They'd considered smashing the box in the compactor, but even if they'd wanted to, he wasn't sure they'd've been able. The building's power died once Asp and Twilight were paste.

There were other ways to destroy it above digital manipulation, though. He could tell the shell wasn't impervious and would likely have been able to end it with a rock, or a long piece of steel wielded like a sledgehammer.

But Ryu did none of those things. He couldn't let go of the mission. Some of what the box had begun feeding them at the pod, on the screens, was the very data they'd gone into this wanting to expose. He could still do what he'd set out to do. He could still tell the world what Xenia and Quark were up to. He could still shift the NAU's power structure before it was too late.

The box's unseen presence in his backpack was a dark and hideous fog all around them. They were headed back to District Zero if they could make it, but still Ryu felt like he was delivering the One Ring to Mordor.

Daemon tapped his temple. "The box. I can hear it inside my head, on my implants."

"Are you sure?"

Daemon nodded.

"What's it saying?"

"Nothing in particular. Just a data dump." But there was a slight pause in there. A sideways tick of the eyes. Seeing it, Ryu knew two things: the box was articulating more than random data, and scaring the bloody hell out of Daemon.

"What are we going to do, boss? I mean … if that ship comes back …"

Somehow the ship didn't worry Ryu. They'd walked past the spot where its blasted crater should have been, and like Twilight said, there was nothing there.

There was, in fact, no evidence at all of the big ship.

So Ryu asked himself: What have we seen of it? I mean, what have we actually, truly experienced? And the answer was: *We saw it on our telemetry. We saw it on our screens.*

They'd all been inside the pod each time the ship appeared, meaning nobody had laid actual human eyes on it. The pod screens were supposed to act like windows, but they were actually digital re-creations of the outside world seen by their external cameras and heard by their external microphones.

Maybe it was one ruse laid atop another.

Maybe, Ryu thought, the ship had never even been.

He didn't tell Daemon. It was a bit crazy … and honestly, the old man had probably already figured it out despite what he'd just said.

"We've got more than five hours. We'll cross that bridge when we come to it."

"Okay, but …"

The question still wasn't answered. Ryu was being a fool, doing exactly what the box — which seemed to have earned its implied intentions and desires — wanted him to. Still, he couldn't let it go. He'd told himself from the start that the mission mattered more than anything. Mitchell had given up a great life to join their team, then surrendered the rest of his existence in their attempt to free the NAU from autocracy. He had known what he was getting into, and so did Ryu.

Yes, the box was dangerous. Yes, it was doing a lot more than calling a ship that might or might not just be a stupid, holographic game. But it was also the codebreaker to end all codebreakers. A magic key, poisonous and homicidal or not.

Ryu had to try, even if it cost his life.

Daemon didn't finish his sentence. Ryu understood fine. They were two bone-weary men with the weight of nine souls on their consciences, carrying their doom like a time bomb with a hot fuse, and they had no way to get anywhere that mattered in the time they were likely to have.

Even without the countdown, The Beam had to know

there was a disturbance at the old industrial park. Even if the box hid it from the wider network, The Beam would notice the black hole in its reconnaissance. Police would come eventually. Or the people who'd made the box, and Ryu was now sure that hadn't been Xenia.

They couldn't stay here and they had no way to get anywhere else. Savage would have described the situation in a syllable: *fucked*.

But then there was a flash on the horizon.

An autocab, pulling up right in front of them.

Ryu clicked the AI into Discussion mode. Not everyone wanted chatter in a cab, but some customers did.

"So," the cab's voice said while they stood outside it, "you guys here on business?"

Daemon and Ryu traded a glance.

Ryu said, "Yeah. We're in software."

"Lovely weather we're having."

"Yes. It's been a warm spring."

"Would you gentlemen like me to drive by the park?"

Ryu shot Daemon another look. "How far away is the park?"

"Just a few minutes. I can—"

Ryu switched the cab back to silent, walked a few paces away, then turned to Daemon. "It's glitched. Still thinks it's in DZ. What the hell's it doing all the way out here?"

Stupid question. It was there for them, of course.

Ryu thought of something else. He walked back to the cab and turned conversation back on.

"Why did you offer to drive us by the park?"

"Because it's lovely this time of year," said the cab.

"But I haven't told you where we're going."

"Pardon, sir, but yes you did."

"Where?"

"To your workshop, sir."

Daemon broke his silence. "I know what you're thinking, but is there any point in not going?"

So they went.

They left the AI conversation on for a while, hoping to milk it for information, but the cab was just a cab other than its far-from-DZ location. It operated like a cab, it rode like a cab, and when they reached DZ the meter clicked on and Ryu saw that it was charging them like a cab. Not that payment was requested. It simply racked up the miles, going about its business, the voice off again once its occupants grew sick of it. The ride bled an hour of time from the clock, then dropped them at the wrong location.

Ryu hadn't noticed. He'd had the cab darken the windows so nobody would see them, but the view outside turned out to have been altered by the software.

Only after exiting the cab did Ryu see that he wasn't at his workshop, or anywhere near it. They were in Chinatown. Across from a Chinese restaurant with a red roof, its doors closed, its windows soaped entirely over.

Daemon was staring at the building. "That's where we're supposed to go."

"What? What makes you say that?" Ryu asked.

Daemon tapped his head.

Ryu considered. Then he moved to cross the street, figuring he might as well peek through the windows.

"Come on," he said, looking back at Daemon.

Daemon shook his head. "That's not a restaurant."

"I know. It's closed. But—"

"It hasn't been a restaurant in a very long time."

Ryu stepped back onto the curb. These weren't guesses or suppositions. Daemon talked like he knew these things.

"The box?"

Daemon nodded.

"What do you see?"

"Quark encryption," Daemon told him, eyeing the restaurant like it might cross the street for him. "It's like what they were using in the Crossbrace days, but a little different. Like two chips off the same block, but not the same as each other."

Ryu took a breath. "Okay. Duly warned. Let's check it out."

He moved again, but this time something different stopped him. Daemon, grabbing him by the backpack.

He turned and Daemon jabbed his pistol into Ryu's ribs. "I'm sorry, boss."

"Daemon, what the hell?"

"I'm sorry, but I can't let you win."

"*Win?*"

"I've seen it," Daemon said, and Ryu knew he was talking about the box's decoded feed, apparently still inside his head.

Ryu's neutered handheld had seen some of that, too. Once they got inside the District Zero core network, it had come alive with new and impossible metrics. The handheld had no connectivity, so what he saw could only be coming from the box.

It was fantastic. Frightening. And full of splendor.

"I've seen how I die," Daemon finished.

"Daemon ..."

"I'm sorry," he said, fishing the straps off of Ryu's shoulders, the gun's aim never wavering. "I'm so sorry, boss, but I don't want to kill you, either."

"Daemon, neither one of us has to—"

"I'm sorry," he said one last time.

And then he ran.

It took Ryu a few seconds to react. He'd just been mugged by his own man — a gifted technologist he'd been working with on and off for more than a decade. This wasn't like Daemon. It was emotional and impulsive. But then again, Daemon *used to be* emotional, before his firewall.

Ryu remembered discussions they'd had, in which Daemon more or less admitted he planned to hide behind it. That he was happier to partition-off his fears and issues rather than face them. Not that his old neuroses had gone away; they'd simply taken a more scientific form. For instance, his primary area of research was life extension. He'd hoped to solve it before his time came because nothing scared Daemon more than the prospect of his life ending.

It seemed the box had known that. It'd found his one remaining emotional weakness.

Ryu ran after him. Daemon was faster than expected — faster than anyone would expect a man his age to be. He pushed through a crowd and was momentarily gone from sight, until Ryu reached and scattered the same crowd.

Daemon's coat flapped around a corner into an alley.

Ryu knew Chinatown well, and where that alley led. Daemon, who'd worked for years in this area, still had contacts. He was probably going after them now, somewhere in the guts of the underground clubs.

There were parties that never stopped in some parts of Chinatown. Raves that went on twenty-four hours a day, fueled by illegal stimulants with its participants hypnotized by feel-good simulations simulcast on flashing screens — psychedelic hedonism immersions so deep in the human subconscious they came off as troubling rather than erotic to those not on drugs.

The basements of those places were filled with old men who quietly ran crime rings, surrounded by bodyguards equipped for direct-to-cortex torture simulations. Daemon had made friends with the seedier elements. Ryu, whose business interests sometimes clashed with theirs, was less welcome.

And now Daemon was taking them the box, just to keep it out of Ryu's hands. Why would Ryu kill Daemon? Why did one of them have to "win"? Ryu wasn't violent unless he had to be. Daemon was about to throw away their mission — and, at the same time, put the box into unstable hands — on a hunch.

Or maybe he planned to destroy it. He'd decided in the end that Twilight was right. He'd been more blank-faced than Ryu, while back at the pod, watching predictions unfurl.

Maybe, in all that data, Daemon had seen something Ryu hadn't.

And Ryu had seen plenty.

Predictions about the direction of Shift.

Predictions about which party — Enterprise or Directorate, led by Micah Ryan or Isaac Ryan — would control the Senate.

Predictions about the ratification of a new currency. Of an unofficial imprint on the Beam. About Noah West's daughter.

But Noah West didn't have a daughter.

Ryu rounded a second corner, into a second and smaller alley.

The buildings were scrunched together, dead-ended ahead in doors Ryu could only pass with the right Beam ID and a willingness to defend himself.

Daemon was ahead, the gap between them closed somewhat but not close enough to tackle.

He shouted. Daemon looked back, then ran harder.

An old Chinese woman grabbed Ryu by the shoulder.

He looked down at her, but she put something in his hands before he could say anything.

"Stop him with this."

She'd handed him a nonlethal weapon designed by Ryu himself, circulated in the underground and now serendipitously set in his own hands.

He looked up and saw the old woman's eyes swim with flecks of light.

Flies in the eyes, Nero would have said.

"Who are you?"

"Hurry. Otherwise everyone else die too."

Ryu ran. He easily held the thing she'd given him in one hand. It was the size of a fat pen and twice as long. It worked similar to NPS nanobots, swarming toward the target and neutralizing their motor neurons. Ryu's paralyzer was more directional, though. It fired fast like a slingshot, not slow like a swarm.

Daemon reached an unmarked door and yanked its handle. He looked back at Ryu, then knocked using a special pattern.

"Who there?" Shouted a voice behind the door.

"I'm a friend."

"You a friend you prove it! Show ID!"

But Daemon couldn't do that. Ryu had purged his own DNA-based Beam ID, but other members of the team weren't willing to cut themselves off so definitively from society forever. In them, Ryu had blocked ID transmission. The effect wore off naturally over time, but for now whoever held the Beam scanner inside the building would be reading Daemon as nothing at all — a vagrant at best.

"My ID is blocked."

"No ID no come in!"

Ryu slowed. He was out of breath, about fifty feet away.

"Daemon. Think about this. Give me the box."

He hugged the backpack closer.

"I won't hurt you. Nobody will. The others got into trouble because they fought. They fought over the box and they fought over each other. That means we know the way out, don't we? We just have to agree." Ryu extended a hand and walked a few steps closer. "Now. Give it to me."

"No."

"It's manipulating you. Don't you see? That's how it got every one of them. It made Chase think Nero was dead when he wasn't, counting on paranoia to make him believe that his lover was a Cleric. It knew Locus lost everything when he lost Smoke, same as he had with his wife."

"Locus was married?"

"*Was.* She died. But remember what Tenor told him? That I was a rat. He said it was my fault Smoke died. Otherwise he'd never have turned, other than to avenge Smoke." Ryu shook his head. "It *knows* us, Daemon. Somehow it knows us better than we know ourselves. Do this and you're falling right into its trap."

Daemon looked like he might hear sense, but fear had blinded him.

There was more alley to go, more doors farther down to try.

He ran. He'd get through one of those doors if Ryu didn't stop him.

The alley was bisected by another one, creating cross-traffic. Daemon pushed through a few milling lowlifes — Lunis junkies low on supply, from the looks of them.

Daemon turned on sudden afterburners, now in a sprint, his eyes on a door that was wide open at its end. He looked back, seemed to again say he was sorry, and barreled toward it.

Ryu tripped. He hit the pavement and his air left him.
"Daemon! Stop!"

But he didn't. And the door beckoned.

The paralyzer.

Ryu looked at his hands. Both were empty. Then he saw the small cylinder the old woman had given him lying not far away on the concrete.

He picked it up, primed it, and took aim.

He had one shot to stop Daemon's muscles. He couldn't reason with the old man, so he'd have to cut him out. With Daemon paralyzed, Ryu would take the backpack and leave him to regain movement in his own time. He'd take the box and do what needed to be done, with or without help.

Ryu aimed. He fired.

Instead of freezing and falling over, Daemon detonated. It was as if the man had swallowed a bomb.

Spatter hit the walls. Clumps flew like scraps from a fireworks display. Something metallic hit the ground just ahead, clotted with red gore. Part of Daemon, or shrapnel from something?

Ryu realized it wasn't metal; it was a flexible implant alloy called Brunellium.

His former friend's mental partition.

He gave himself exactly one second to wallow in guilt and mourning.

Then Ryu ran into the mess and retrieved the backpack.

Because now it was speaking to him.

Chapter Fourteen

THE BOX

Ryu had seen the default canvas avatar a thousand times. This one was somehow different. It wasn't blankly compliant like they typically were, looking only to serve. Instead it was upright and strong, projecting arrogance no avatar ever could.

He watched, wondering how many of his faculties were still his own. Ryu didn't really remember returning to this place — not as his own body's pilot, anyway.

He remembered traipsing through the gore that had once been Daemon only as a visitor to his senses, discovering he could find no pieces of the man larger than a finger. The backpack was blood-soaked but intact. Whatever the weapon had done to his old collaborator wasn't something Ryu had seen before.

It vaporized the man ... but *only* the man. Daemon's clothes were right there in a pile, shirt arms still threaded through the backpack straps. The thing he'd shot at Daemon certainly wasn't the paralyzer he'd believed it to be. The woman had handed him something entirely different, and he hadn't thought twice. He'd been too preoccupied with the idea that the box was manipulating Daemon into running that it never occurred to him that it might be manipulating Ryu into pursuit.

He hadn't known the thing would kill Daemon … Ryu was almost certain of that. He hadn't thought it strange that a random woman would hand him a weapon, knowing what he was after; he hadn't thought it odd that she was a Cleric; he hadn't put any of that together and decided maybe he shouldn't shoot what she had given without testing it first.

The box was to blame. Ryu thought he was doing the right thing. Never mind that he'd gotten exactly what he wanted, no matter the price.

The avatar shimmered. It looked so solid, only after the shimmer did Ryu remember that he wasn't looking at a flesh-and-blood man.

"I don't know how I got here," Ryu told the avatar. The mindless piece of software. *Here* was inside the red-roofed Chinese restaurant with the soaped-over windows.

Inside, the place was anything but an eatery. It was something between a lab and a convalescent's bedroom. There was a large bed against one wall, surrounded by IV racks and unplugged monitoring equipment. On the other end was a long bench filled with tech that struck Ryu as old but still unseen — unreleased inventions from a genius creator, perhaps, discovered only now.

"The nanobots assisted you in coming here," said the avatar. "They came from the weapon you fired."

"Daemon," Ryu said.

"Daemon. Yes. There were great hopes for Daemon. If it hadn't been you, it likely would have been him."

"I killed him," Ryu said, toneless.

The avatar nodded. "You didn't mean to, though … did you?"

Ryu liked hearing that. He decided to make it true. He sat in a rolling chair pulled from the room's edge, rattling the casters in the big open space.

"Why am I here?"

"To help someone who needs it."

"Do I have a choice?"

"Everyone always has a choice."

"But the nanobots …"

"The nanobots kept your legs moving. It was necessary. You couldn't stay where you were. Even in this part of town, liquifying a person draws attention."

"So you can make me do whatever you want."

The avatar sat. The chair was real and the avatar was a hologram, but the illusion was entirely convincing. "Not you. Never you. Not the great Ryu."

"So you know me."

"I know your abilities. I know your ambition and apti-tude. I know that you are the best. And I know you take great precautions. Your mental shielding, for one, plus all the redundant false-neuron circuitry you installed in your brain and body. That must have been painful."

It was. Ryu had needed to do it all himself, and that meant he could only use local pain-blockers. Needing motor control meant he couldn't block all the pain. That was fine. Ryu was used to sacrifice in the name of the greatest good.

"Oh, the box could take over one of your arms at a time, I'm sure," the avatar went on, "but the other would keep cycling, fed through alternate pathways, and it would be a pain in the ass. If the device wanted something it could completely control, it would have used an armature. Or a Cleric. But it requires more than hands, Ryu. It needs your mind. Your skills. Those are things that cannot be forced."

Ryu saw the box. He'd taken it out of the soiled back-pack and set it on the workbench. He remembered that now, through his haze.

He stood and walked to the worktable. "I could pick this up."

"You could."

"But I can't destroy it."

"I'm sure you could. Eventually you'll need to open it up."

"*Open* it?"

"How else could you work? How else could you do with it what needs to be done?"

Ryu touched the box, the way they had before. No countdown displayed on its surface. No note of its itera-tions. Instead, its side lowered like the door of an oven. The thing was filled with circuitry that was fine and deli-cate and beautiful, like art made of gossamer. He could ruin it. Now that its hard case was open, he could break it with the softest of breaths.

"Who are you?" Ryu asked.

"Not who you think I am."

"So you *are* an avatar." The factory default on every Quark-made canvas and terminal created since 2063. Arguably the most famous face of all time, because unless the user changed it (and many didn't bother) it was the face of The Beam itself.

"What you see is a shell filled with a construct," said the avatar. "The construct was aggregated from the files and public appearances and private records of a person. I am what that man seemed to be, but I am not the man himself. You can think of me as an impersonator, not the person."

"Of who?"

"Ryu. Please. You've figured this out. You know the answer, or you wouldn't be here."

"No." He shook his head.

"You should be honored. Out of all the people considered, you were the best. Don't be coy, Ryu. We wouldn't be here if my software didn't know this was a puzzle you'd want to solve." The avatar leaned forward. "It's tempting, isn't it?"

"What is?"

"Immortality."

"You're not immortal," Ryu said. "You're not even real."

The avatar sat back and said, "Not yet."

Immortality.

It was what Ryu had been most afraid of.

But the avatar was right; it once again knew Ryu as well as he knew himself.

This wasn't immortality of the elite Beau Monde or immortality of the powerful at the dying expense of the disenfranchised masses. This was like solving one of the world's greatest puzzles — the way the first cloners must have felt, when upon realizing they could play God.

Ryu was sorely tempted, and torn in every direction at once.

"Say it." Ryu swallowed. "I need to hear you say it."

"Noah West is inside the box."

Ryu had known that was the answer, but hearing it made his chest want to hum like a tuning fork slapped against the wall. *Noah West.* The father of The Beam — creator of Crossbrace, founder of Quark — had been dead going on four decades now, but his presence in the nation had only grown stronger since his passing.

Copies of Noah (really just AI tinged with his public personality) were on every block, inside every building. His memory had spawned a religion. An all-out church. There'd always been people who said Noah West never really died, but people said the same thing about Hitler and Elvis. Conspiracy theorists claimed there'd been a massive encrypted upload on the day of his physical death — something nut jobs and anthroposophists said was Noah's line uploading to The Beam.

Of course it'd been searched and searched, to no avail. There was too much turbulent data on The Beam, and whatever Noah might have squirted into its stream would have blown apart like water dumped into a raging river. It was a theory for crazy people — people who wanted to believe there were literal gods in the machine.

But it wasn't true.

Except that Ryu, who'd seen what the box could do, now believed every bit of it.

"Why should I help you?"

"*Him.* Not me. I'm a software aggregate, here to guide you. Noah himself is — pardon the term — 'Some assembly required.'"

"That's why nobody found him on The Beam. He was scattered into fragments."

"He would say 'diversified.' That was his goal — to be everywhere at once. To have many options, never relying on only one person."

"I'm just one person," said Ryu.

"Yes," said the avatar. "You are."

They stared at one another. It was hard to believe it wasn't a real person sitting across from him.

"You haven't answered my question. Why should I help him? Why shouldn't I destroy this thing right now?"

Ryu moved his hand closer to the delicate circuitry. He threaded his fingers through it, convinced after all the tricks the box had pulled that he needed insurance.

The avatar, if it could be bothered, did not seem to be. Just like the real Noah West, in all those old news clips, always seemed so imperturbable. The avatar had Noah's surety. His smug way of sitting back with hands folded, convinced he was superior to any possible opposition and could win any encounter without lifting a finger.

Ryu half-wanted to prove the avatar wrong.

The box thought it could control Ryu? *Nothing* controlled Ryu.

"Because it's the greatest puzzle of all time. Noah's mental imprint is scattered across The Beam in a billion pieces, and the box is the map required to reassemble them. But it's not just instructions, you know. I've seen what Xenia is up to; I've been reading up the entire time your friends have been busy dying. Xenia can't solve Mindbender because it doesn't know where a person's true being really lives. It's not in his elements. It's not in the bonds between his atoms, nor in the synapses between the nerves in his brain. It's a problem too big for mechanistic thinking. Only Noah really understood, though Xenia will eventually get there. You can destroy the matter and map its reassembly, but a vessel is still required for *him*." The avatar indicated the box. "You've been carrying around a part of him. A bit like a soul."

"You orchestrated this."

The avatar shook his head. "Noah did. Years ago."

"How did he know? It's been so long."

"The universe is just math, Ryu. You know that. Events were too far out for certainty, but the tendencies were all there. I have most of his logic. I can stay current. And Noah has always had friends. The return of Noah West will change The Beam. Those who helped him will earn their favor when it happens."

"You make it sound Faustian. Like a deal with the devil."

"I predicted you'd feel that way." The avatar laughed. "Good old righteous Ryu. Social crusader Ryu. You want everyone to get along. You care about equal opportunity."

"That's right," said Ryu, now gripping the fragile wires. The avatar still hadn't reacted — certainly not with alarm.

"So rather than fame and power, I have something else to offer you in exchange."

"What?"

"That which you wished in the first place. Noah has no need for Xenia. Quark had spiraled in his absence; he has no need for current-day Quark, either. The hierarchical divide that scares you so much means nothing to him. Noah wanted human advancement. He *wants* human advancement," the avatar corrected. "Your goal of exposing the secrets is one he shares. Assemble the puzzle. Re-imbue Noah's pieces with the repository of his soul. When it's done, the box will be at your command. You may use it to undermine any power structures you wish."

"That's what we thought the first time," Ryu said.

"You were incorrect. This time, you are not."

"It was all just a game, wasn't it? The countdown meant nothing. There was no black ship. The chase was just keeping us busy."

"It was a test. A kind of audition. You were given puzzles to solve, to see how you reacted. Noah requires certain qualities. Whoever was to assist him would need skills, cunning, agile thinking, and a level head. That person needed to focus on the right things and ignore the wrong ones, even under intense, ever-changing pressure and mortal threat."

"So you killed them all. For a goddamn *audition*."

The avatar shook its head. "They killed themselves. They killed each other."

"The box opened the door behind Chase. It dropped Twilight and Asp into the compactor."

"Chase was volatile. He took a hostage. Twilight and Asp fought to the death. All architects of their own demise."

"But the box gave them a push."

"Yes, Ryu. You are correct. Is that all it takes, to turn good people bad? *A push?*"

His hand slackened on the wires. It was true, if still wrong. The box hadn't made things wrong. It had simply given them a venue in which to make fatal mistakes.

He could do this. He *should* do this. Noah's avatar was right; the lure of the legendary technological riddle was almost too much to resist.

Beyond that, the problems with Xenia and Mindbender and all the rest remained. If Ryu walked out now, he would have solved nothing. The world would still die.

But if he did as the avatar wished and helped put Noah's genie back in its bottle, chances were the real Noah West would keep Mindbender technology all to himself. West wanted to impress the world, not truly empower it. He wanted to accomplish remarkable things, but never allow those accomplishments to eclipse their maker. Mindbender had followed his death — spurred in part by rumors about the circumstances of Noah's passing — specifically because it wasn't something he would have ever permitted while alive.

Gods in the machine? Not for anyone other than the great Noah West.

Maybe it really was the best way. West hated competition and being usurped. Simply being absent from the world for so long had left him expropriated by default.

He'd want to raze the playing field and start over, and none of the casualties would be people or entities or sectors Ryu cared to save. They might even work together to right the world's ship. Noah would want to be a god, sure, but maybe that was okay. Maybe Ryu could sit at the right hand of that god, guiding its direction.

Could it possibly be worse than what would happen if he refused?

Ryu's eyes went to his hand. The hand slowly emerged from the box, careful not to disturb the circuitry on its way out. Wires gave way to a view of his own soft human flesh. So fragile, in itself.

The ring on his finger glinted in the space's flat light. The ring a friend had given him, because she alone had wanted freedom from the system as badly as Ryu did.

"What about Savage?" he asked as the ring held his attention.

The avatar puzzled. "What *about* Savage?"

"Rogue and Smoke died in a firefight, trying to steal things that didn't belong to us. Then it was Locus and Tenor, who you 'pushed' into trying to take over and maybe execute me as a traitor. Chase and Nero were volatile — Chase willing to take hostages and Nero hiding secrets. Twilight pulled a gun on us. Asp pulled a gun on Twilight. Daemon was going to take the box to the Chinese mafia to save his own neck. Even I put this all together, responsible for the lot of them."

Ryu leaned toward the man that wasn't really there. "But tell me about Savage, if you've got it all 'decrypted.' Tell me why she deserved to die. She was only trying to help. She believed in the ideals of this venture more than anyone else. She wasn't even going to take a full share of the money — just enough to get by. You know why that was? Because Savage couldn't live with herself if she might think later that she had only done it for the payday."

"Savage was collateral damage. All of you were profiled to discover weaknesses that might pose a problem. She had her weakness as well. You were all poised to break. You, Ryu, were the only one who didn't."

"Collateral damage," Ryu repeated.

"An accident. Could not be helped."

But that was a lie.

The avatar already said it was all just a test. An audition. Anyone who wasn't good enough had to go, because if Noah West had quirks during his life, a few of them were paranoia, secrecy, and an icy demeanor that wrote off bad (even illegal) behavior as the cost of achievement.

Like all world-changers, Noah West was both beloved and venomously hated.

In life and death, the man was both hero and villain.

Noah West wouldn't allow more than one person to survive this. There were always going to be ten corpses and one accomplice.

Something shifted within Ryu. His eyes rose, and when the avatar saw them, something new entered its artificial intelligence.

"You say we all had our weaknesses."

The avatar nodded.

"What was Savage's?"

"Idealism. An intense, blinding obsession with the mission."

"You're saying she cared too much."

"You could say that."

"Ironic."

The avatar looked puzzled. "What's ironic?"

"It's just that maybe she'd've been a better winner of this thing than me."

"What do you mean?"

"I just decided." Ryu shrugged. "I don't care at all."

"What're you—?" the avatar demanded.

It stopped when Ryu shoved his hand into the box and ripped out its guts.

The avatar blipped from existence.

Ryu went to the door, which was, of course, locked.

"Brennan," he said to the door. "Are you there?"

"Yes, Mr. Ryu," came a voice from the outside.

"You got my message."

"The nanobots interpreted a message, sir, using the parameters you set."

"Can you open the door?"

The door opened and Brennan was standing in front of him, looking more or less the same as he had the last time Ryu had asked him to animate. That was … what? Six months ago, when they'd all had dinner? Brennan had done a great job waitering that day — enough that Ryu considered keeping him online all the time.

He wasn't a Cleric; he was a cyborg, so it wasn't like Ryu would have to worry about true sentience unless he wanted it to develop. But it also meant that Brennan wasn't aware when he was in storage, and didn't mind all that time blacked out. Ryu didn't need a servant. It made him feel like he was part of the problem rather than part of the solution.

Ryu exhaled.

"Are you all right, sir?"

"I was worried the door wouldn't open. This is Quark we're talking about." He looked back at the ripped-apart box, its wires like spilled innards. Then at the chair, where Noah's avatar had been.

He didn't need to tell Brennan about that. Or anyone.

"The nanobots have been with you the entire time as

requested, sir. I daresay they learned a few tricks about encryption from watching the box." Then Brennan noticed the box. "Oh dear. Were you able to decrypt the Xenia files before it was broken?"

"I'll find another way," Ryu answered.

"If you don't mind, sir …?"

"What is it, Brennan?"

"What *was* the box?"

Ryu looked at it one more time. "Junk."

Brennan nodded.

"Did you bring the swarm?"

Brennan pulled a small reservoir of nanos from his pocket. Unlike the other swarm cans, this one was bright red. *Scavengers*.

Ryu pointed at the box. "Leave nothing."

Chapter Fifteen

NOAH

THIRTY-FIVE YEARS EARLIER

Noah looked at the cube on his bedside table. The woman beside him was entering values into a decision matrix, trying to shore up informational holes. The new network had begun to hum beneath the old one, and had already surpassed his dying expectations. The growth of The Beam, once deployed across the nation, would be exponential — and Noah for one was sure there'd soon be no need to enter any values manually because there would *be* no informational holes.

Crossbrace's adoption was near-total. The Beam would surpass that, once people saw for themselves the ways it would change things.

His eyes went to the cube again. The thing looked like granite, but the fiber inside was spiderweb thin. Keep it closed and it'd handle like a tank. Only the intended engineers would ever be able to open the thing.

He returned his attention to the woman. She'd put a screen on the wall, near where Stephen York usually sat.

York, who'd remained a faithful partner to Noah even at his own expense, believed he was the only other person to enter the Chinatown workshop.

But York was incorrect. Whenever he ran out for something (food, water, entertainment, or the abundant medical supplies required for his slowly withering body), Noah brought in his technicians. Someone different every time, and a swarm of neuro-adaptive nanos hovering outside the front door erased all memory of their visits.

He could have used York for this, but Noah's subordinate would be responsible for the upload of Noah's consciousness in his final dying days. He might flake out. He might get cold feet, worried about the morality of uploading his superior's mind to The Beam.

But he could never — *should* never — put too much trust in one person. He had to diversify. Noah needed a few things to go his way or this would never work, but he'd built in enough failsafes that he thought he'd be okay.

Even if York chickened out, the redundant uploads he'd been making over time would cobble together enough of a "Noah imprint" that his consciousness would probably still manage to find his center.

His consciousness, on the other hand, had proven to function a little like a hologram. One piece of a broken hologram provided blueprints enough for the whole thing. So it was with Noah's "soul," if that's what he wanted to call it. He'd make a few copies, then nudge them to a few different sets of hands. Only one copy had to survive, then mate with the raw data scattered across The Beam.

The thought made him look to the far end of York's bench, where three identical cubes were waiting. This final tech would take all four cubes with her, put them into play, then promptly forget all she had done — or even that she had met the legendary Noah West.

And there the cubes would sit until certain other machinations came into play, probably decades from now, triggered once the network matured fully enough to support his re-integration and return.

One cube would have to stay with Xenia, probably earmarked for Killian's son if he stayed with the company. One would go to Quark, though Noah assumed his company would turn its collective back on their founder and fearless leader once he was dead. One would go into the underground, where hackers and technologists would compete for it in orchestrated auditions, weeding through candidates until it found the best of them to assist his endeavor. And the other was his backup. Hopefully it would never be needed.

Each step of the way required human hands, but Noah doubted they'd all desert him. If Rachel Ryan wouldn't help him return, for instance, the odds were good that one of her power-hungry sons would.

"Finished," said the woman.

Noah looked at the screen. "Will it work?"

"The boxes?"

"The plan as a whole."

She knew he meant the predictive matrices, but Noah's question was pointless. Still, he wanted to ask.

"It's too far out. At this level of system maturity, the math can really only predict a few hours ahead."

"General tendencies, then."

The woman considered the data, wheeling the display's timeframe to its maximum. The solid, certain lines of real time data gave way quickly to lines so fuzzy, they were barely there. And this was only a few weeks, not the decades Noah wanted to see.

"The trajectory seems correct," said the tech. "Probability that all four boxes will survive into their temporary locations looks excellent. I see no reason to doubt the people you either already have in positions of trust or those you will bring in later."

"If it showed that the people I bring in later were unreliable, would I be able to choose different people?"

"Are you asking me if destiny exists, or if the future can be changed?"

Noah shrugged. He felt decent today, despite his terminal diagnosis. Time to be playful. Time to ask the big questions, just because he could.

"That's one for the philosophers, I'm afraid," she said.

"Will one of the four boxes be deployed intact?"

"It's too far out. I can't say."

"Best guess."

"Too far out, Mr. West. I'm sorry."

"What can you tell me?"

"Your upload will likely complete. York will do as you wish."

"Of course he will." Noah had been soft on that prediction earlier, so hearing near certainty was an overwhelming relief. Stephen was brilliant, but spineless. The man had never been able to disobey.

"He will regret it when it's finished."

"Regret?"

"At least moral quandary. Soul-searching. Wondering if he's done the right thing."

Noah laughed. "I don't need a predictive matrix to tell me that about Stephen."

The tech smiled, unsure of what to say next.

"So I'll live on. At least in some form."

The woman nodded. "Disembodied as data, yes. I imagine you'll have some level of awareness that way, but not a whole lot. Even that's a guess."

"And if I'm re-integrated? If one of the boxes survives and ends up deployed?"

"Then I suppose you're all the way back, sir."

His head bobbed. It was as good as he was going to get, as far as assurances of immortality were concerned.

"And this is interesting." The woman stopped just as she prepared to close the screen. "This new line here is gaining in certainty as I'm watching it. I can't say where it will go, other than 'away.'"

"What do you mean, 'It's going away'?"

She considered, then shook her head. "Can't say. She's going to leave the network and disappear, is all I can say for mostly-sure. For a very long time. Into the mountains? If you want to, once you're back, you can probably use this same matrix to find exactly where she is. It'll have a lot more data by then."

But there was an assumption here that Noah didn't have — a piece of the tech's prediction that made zero sense.

"Who's *she*?" Noah didn't have any women left in his life anymore. The line onscreen was so bold and clear, it had to be an *important* woman, too, not someone insignificant like Carol from the Quark board. Noah couldn't think of anyone who fit the bill. He had no family.

The woman looked amused when she turned to face him. "Your daughter, of course."

He blinked. "I don't have a daughter."

Her smile fell, seeing his puzzlement. She glanced again at the screen, then looked Noah in the eyes.

"You do, sir," she said. "You didn't know?"

The End...

ONE BOX WAS NOT ENOUGH.

Noah Fucking West: that's the swear the world dedicated to the architect of The Beam after his questionable death. West has been dead for decades, but some say he'll one day return, possibly with the help of other boxes Ryu was unable to find in time … and that the omniscient, omnipresent network he birthed has been saving a place for him at life's table. If you liked this book, it's just an appetizer to Platt & Truant's most epic story world: *The Beam*, in which humanity slides ever closer to digital oblivion, becoming less human all along the way. Read on in *The Beam*, available now.

You've just read *Future Proof,* a stand-alone prequel in the world of *The Beam* ... but *The Beam* is our biggest world and there's so much more to read.

First things first: **If by some chance you got to this book without reading the core *Beam* series, you need to read that next FO SHO.** You can get it from the usual bookstores, but it's cheapest at JohnnyBTruant-Books.com.

But then, after that, there are these bombshells:

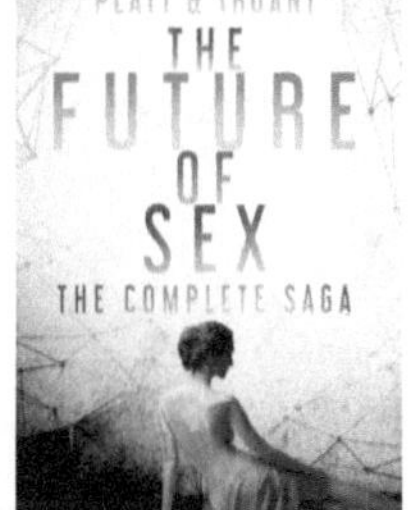

THE FUTURE OF SEX: Read the Origin of Chloe Shaw

Chloe was always a prodigy, able to command The Beam and understand it in ways others never could. She thought she was just an escort, but it turned out she was the One the world had been waiting for.

***The Future of Sex* is an epic 12-book series available in a single omnibus.**

Enter the Truantverse

When it comes to stories and the worlds they live in, books are only the beginning.

Visit JohnnyBTruant.com/join to get my best books sooner and cheaper than the other stores.

My list doesn't suck like so many author email lists. Seriously. It has unicorns.

The Unforgotten

The Magic Bunch

Unicorn Genesis

❧

FAT VAMPIRE:

Fat Vampire

Fat Vampire 2: Tastes Like Chicken

Fat Vampire 3: All You Can Eat

Fat Vampire 4: Harder Better Fatter Stronger

Fat Vampire 5: Fatpocalypse

Fat Vampire 6: Survival of the Fattest

The Vampire Maurice

Anarchy and Blood

Vampires in the White City

Fangs and Fame

Game of Fangs

❧

INVASION:

Invasion

Contact

Colonization

Annihilation

Judgment

Extinction

Resurrection

Save the City

Save the Girl

Save the World

Longshot

THE INEVITABLE:

Robot Proletariat

The Infinite Loop

The Hard Reset

Cascade Failure

Reboot

En3my

THE INEVITABLE:

DEAD CITY:

Dead City

Dead Nation

Dead Planet

Dead Zero

Empty Nest

THE DREAM ENGINE:

The Dream Engine

The Nightmare Factory

The Ruby Room

The Pandora Core

The Engine Convergence

The Tinkerer's Mainspring

GORE POINT:

Gore Point 1

Gore Point 2

Gore Point 3

THE BEAM:

The Beam: Season One

The Beam: Season Two

The Beam: Season Three

The Beam Season Four

The Beam Season Five

Future Proof

Plugged

The Future of Sex

THE TOMORROW GENE:

The Tomorrow Gene

The Eden Experiment

The Tomorrow Clone

Null Identity

COMEDIES:

Everyone Gets Divorced

Greens

Fiends

Decoy Wallet

NONFICTION:

The Fiction Formula

Fiction Unboxed

Iterate & Optimize

The Story Solution

Write. Publish. Repeat.

The One With All the Writing Advice